Surrounded by Death and Destruction

The Diary of Emelise Carson

OLIVIA M. OBRINGER

Galveston, Texas

1900

Friday, August 24, 1900

A blank book filled with wonderful, cream-colored pages, just waiting for me to write down every single thought I will ever have. And to think I was going to wander about in town, ignoring my mother's order to clean the attic! What would have become of this new diary then?

Let me start over. Mother insisted I clean the filthy attic today and make it "just as clean as the rest of the house is going to be."

"The attic?" I wailed. "Why can't Anthony do it?"

"Anthony is tending to his rabbits while you are just standing there. Go."

Only then out of the corner of my eye did I see Papa walking down the street, the right side of his body falling with each stride because of his limping. His head turned left and right, I could see, as he took in his surroundings. He was going to town! For the first time since being here for three days, Papa was going to walk around town—without me!

I thought to sneak out the backdoor, but Mother read my mind and declared, "If you even *think* of going with your father to walk around Galveston, you will have no supper tonight, young lady!"

I wanted to say back, "So? It's only one meal," but decided against it. I stomped up the stairs to the attic, only to walk into a spider web first thing. But if I *hadn't* walked into that spider web, I never would have sat down on the wooden crate and caught a glance of this little, brown book peeking out from under the bureau.

Wait, I hear Mother coming up the stairs, calling, "Emelise! Emelise! Are you cleaning the attic?"

I must hurry and hide this diary.

Five minutes later...

Note to self: never show a mother your diary.

Mother opened the door as soon as I closed this book. She set her hands on her hips like she always does and said, "What is that?"

"My diary. I found it."

"Let me see."

I reluctantly handed it to her, and she glanced through the first page, her eyes moving back and forth with each line she read.

"Tsk, tsk."

"What?" I thought she was going to grow angry with my writing about her.

"Really, Emelise, you shouldn't fiddle with unnecessary trifles." Her delicate hands gestured in the air, as if she were mute and needed to use her hands to speak just as she needed to use her mouth. I didn't pay much attention to my mother's lecture, but watched her as she rattled on about me being too old for diaries. Her hair was still neat and in order, despite the constant work the family has been doing since the move. I think I even spotted some rouge rubbed into her face. *Strange*, I thought. Mother never wears blush unless going somewhere. But, as she *always* says, "We need to look our best and impress people here." I wonder how smoothing red blush on our cheeks can increase our popularity and ability to earn friends.

Mother had stopped speaking, and her silky-smooth fingers were fiddling with the blue diamond necklace. She expected me answer.

"How is it childish?" I blurted out, hoping that question made sense to what she had been saying. "It's writing, and writing increases my penmanship."

Of course, Mother never answered me and just tossed

the book back in my lap and walked down the stairs, calling, "Hurry and clean the attic! I have more for you to do." My thoughts? I don't think she had an answer.

Now I have to clean the attic. Ugh. There are spider webs in every corner, near every rafter. I can't even walk without the dreadful awareness of having traipsed through another one. Not to mention how many boxes litter the area. Some are stacked on top of each other and they soar higher than I am tall. And the dust. Goodness, do I hate dust. It must be two inches thick in some areas. When I saw this diary under the bureau I closed my eyes and pretended to touch something else, but I am pretty darn sure a spider had scurried across my hand. Or maybe it was a mouse. Nevertheless, this place is a mess, and it is going to take forever to clean it up. I don't even know why Mother has me do this; no one *dines* in the attic.

Oh, no. I hear her coming up the stairs again. I need to put this diary away and try to make it look like I am making progress.

After cleaning the attic...

I am outside now, sitting by the rabbit hut. Mother did not notice when I slipped out the door. Anthony is who-knows-where, and Samuel is probably with him, since those two never leave each other's side. I am sitting alone.

I just looked back to what I wrote so far, and what a bad way to start off a brand new diary! I never stated who I was, where I live, my family—nothing!

Let me start off with who I am. My name is Emelise Lillian Carson, and I just turned thirteen on August 3. I have dark hair that is in a side braid at the moment, and big blue eyes. Papa says I sometimes look like an owl with my large eyes. My nose is small, and one of my worst features is that I have a two inch scar on the right part of my neck. When I was three, Papa told me, I decided to cut my long, beautiful hair for whatever reason. When I did, I accidentally missed my hair and cut my neck. The scar has never completely vanished.

We moved from Little Rock, Arkansas, to here, and I now live on 23rd Street in Galveston, Texas. The city of Galveston is on Galveston Island, two miles off the coast of the real Texas state. There are about 38,000 people living in the city of Galveston alone!

We moved here to be closer to Alice—the best sister in the world. Alice is twenty-two years old. She finished college a few years ago, and then went to *another* school to become a Catholic Sister. Since she has summers off the Sisters and Nuns in charge of her school sent her here, to Galveston, where she can volunteer at St. Mary's Orphan Asylum until she must go back and continue her schooling.

I was thrilled to move to Galveston, I must say. Yes, I miss dear Kate, my best friend in the whole world, but to see the best *sister* is even better.

Let me describe me big family now in case when I die someone finds this diary and wonders about my family.

My papa, James Edward Carson, has dark brown hair, which is parted and swooshed over the left side. He wears glasses when reading, and he has gray eyes. One part that I must write down—though I hate recalling that day—was when my papa was in an accident five years ago. It was horrible. Papa was trying out the new horse he was going to buy when somehow it had gotten spooked and threw him right in the path of an oncoming wagon. People didn't really do anything for the longest time, only stared as he lay crumpled on the street. I was there. I know.

But the people all the sudden awoke from their slumber and rushed towards him, calling a doctor, all the while me crying and screaming.

I remember every detail of that day: the blood leaking

through the cracks in the street, Papa mumbling, very faintly, "Emelise, don't cry," and the way the doctor had a worried look on his face when he saw Papa for the first time.

I wish I could forget, like the way I forget to do the daily cleaning, but it seems to be stuck in my head. Why do all the bad memories stay in my brain but the good ones go in and out?

He did recover, after months, but he did not recover fully. His arms and face are covered in scars, and he walks with a limp, but he is still handsome and I have gotten so used to the scars that I hardly notice them now.

Papa is kind with us, and hardly ever grows frustrated, except, of course, with Edward. But I will get to *him* later.

Next is Mother. She is one year younger than father. She has brown hair, like me, that she wears up in a bun during the day. Ringlets cover her ears—"Your ears should *always* be covered," she tells me—and she has blue eyes. Mother married Papa at age twenty-two—the same age Alice is now—and moved away from Grandpa Lucas and Grandma Ann in Massachusetts to Arkansas with Papa. I think Mother favors her sons more than she does me. She talks with Anthony and Samuel nicely, while with me she is snapping every chance she gets—at least I think so. I told Nathan this one time, and he disagreed, saying Mother loves each of us equally. I am not so sure.

Alice Esther is the first child and, oh, what a good young lady she is! My sister has sort of *frizzy* brown hair, blue eyes, a curved nose, and a small chin. I haven't seen her in years, so maybe she doesn't even have frizzy hair anymore. Maybe her chin grew larger. My sister is the best listener. She is quiet, I must say, but that is because she is always caring for others and doesn't really need to say anything.

Now Alice is training to become a Catholic Sister (didn't I say she was holy?). She volunteers—as I mentioned before—at an orphanage right here in Galveston! I wanted to visit her right away, and I know everyone else did too, but

Mother said we needed to unpack and get acquainted with the town, and then we could have her over for dinner on Sunday. I think Mother must be crazy. How does she, for one, expect me to grow *acquainted* with the town if she won't let me outside?! And having my own sister "over for dinner" sounds so formal. But I guess I can wait until Sunday, for it is only two days away.

Edward Lawrence is the second child. Ugh. I hate even saying his name. He is seventeen years old and more stubborn than me. He and Papa get in so many fights—mostly over Ruth Henry, his *sweetheart* back in Little Rock. Edward wants to go back there to her, but Papa forbids it—even though Ruth is the sweetest young lady—because Edward needs to finish school. Papa says when Edward finishes college he can move back to Little Rock, only Edward is worried Ruth will fall for someone else.

One time I asked him, "Why are you afraid? Don't you think you are handsome enough?"

I will never forget the way his jaw fell open like that and how is eyes flashed fire. He said, all full of himself, "Oh, shut up, Emelise." I never told Papa he said this, or else Edward will get in more trouble, which would get *me* in trouble.

But if I were Edward, I *would* worry about him being handsome enough for Ruth. He has brown hair with light brown mixed in here and there. His nose is far too pointy and with his gray eyes, well, I think he looks rather dark and scary instead of bright and cheery. He is not good-looking like Nathan.

Nathan Kenneth is the best brother in the world. He is fifteen years old and has light brown hair that is parted in the middle and slightly curled upward at the tips. He has hazel eyes and is very handsome. There is only one problem—Nathan is semi-sightless. He can see shapes, and he says everything is sort of brown. I know he wishes he could see fully, although he never acts that way. He is very kind and a very good listener. I have told Nathan things I have never told anyone else, not even my best friend. I have told him my fears and goals, and he understands and gives great advice. Who could ask for a better brother? He is very smart, like me. Nathan never complains, and I know Mother appreciates that she has one child who can do work without protesting.

My hand feels as though it is going to fall off from writing so much, so I will write about Anthony and Samuel later.

Before I help Mother with supper...

Mother will be calling me soon, so I will jot down a few things about Anthony and Samuel.
 Anthony Herbert is an eight year old with light brown/blond hair, brown eyes, and freckles. He is tall and skinny, like a telephone pole, I like to say. Anthony talks a lot, which is one bad thing about him out of many.
 Samuel Curtis is six years old, has dark brown hair, and dark, dark brown eyes which are almost black. He is quiet, like Alice, and mostly follows Anthony around. Those two are stuck together like two peas in a pod. Even worse, they both wear a dull red handkerchief around their necks so they can "act like twins."
 Samuel calls Anthony *Herby* while Anthony calls Samuel *Curt*. I absolutely hate it when they say those names in public, but there is no stopping them.
 One thing that I wish we could have left back in Arkansas is the rabbits. The boys—that is what I call Anthony and Samuel—have three Californian rabbits. Papa had to make a cage for them so we could take them on the train "only if you promise to hide them under the seat" the conductor had said. He was really nice, which is why he let the rabbits stay with us.
 It's not that I hate the rabbits themselves; it's just that I

hate catching them. Back in Arkansas they were in a five foot long cage that sat directly on the dirt. They would dig their way out and escape, running all over the yard. Anthony would run in the house screaming bloody murder, "The rabbits have escaped again!" and order us to come help him catch them. It took hours and hours. I was usually the one who had to help them the most because Mother doesn't like to run, Edward would declare he was busy, and Nathan would try to help but, of course, he can't see. Papa would catch the first one, and leave the rest up to me. *That* is why I hate those rabbits so much. They have escaped more times than I can count, and Anthony and Samuel refuse to put plywood on the bottom of the hut because "they like to feel the dirt, and they might get a splinter!"

Even here in Galveston they reject having wood placed on the dirt floor of the hut. There *was* grass, but the rabbits chewed that down quicker than you can say *apple cider*. They are behind the house now, right next to Mother's flower garden.

Mother is calling.

Bedtime...

Supper was grand, with roasted duck, sweet potatoes, corn, cabbage salad, and peach pie. I had two slices, although Mother insisted I will gain weight "eating that way all the time."

Once the table was cleared, everyone went about their own business: Papa reading the paper, Mother dusting, Edward writing a love letter to you-know-who, Nathan practicing the piano, and Anthony and Samuel playing checkers. I wanted to write in this new diary, but Papa claimed he had an announcement to make before I could sneak away.

He set down the paper and cleared his throat. Everyone

stopped what they were doing and turned towards him.

"I was walking around town a little bit today, seeing the houses and businesses, and I decided that it isn't any fun to see your new home without some company."

"You mean we get to go to town tomorrow?" I exclaimed, already clapping my hands in joy.

"Yes." Everyone cheered; that is, everyone except Mother.

"Oh, James. Tomorrow? But there is plenty to do around here. Can't that wait?"

Papa bit his lip, glancing from his wife to his overly excited children. "It will only be a little while, Lillian. No more than a couple of hours."

"But if Alice notices how dirty the house is on Sunday…"

"She won't, Mother," Nathan insisted, grabbing his cane and standing, facing where her voice had come from. "Already the house smells better than a bottle of France's finest perfume."

Mother blushed. She always blushes when she gets compliments from Nathan.

"All right, Nathan, if you want to go that badly, we can."

I wanted to tell Mother that I was the one who wanted to walk around town the most, but, of course, she acted as though Nathan had been the one begging for days.

"Then it's settled," Papa declared. "Tomorrow, everyone dress in their finest clothes. We want to make a good impression on the people of Galveston."

Anthony and Samuel just walked in my bedroom, their handkerchiefs still tied around their necks.

"Emmie?"

"What is it, Anthony?" I asked, angry. "Can't you see I'm busy?"

"I'm scared. My room is really big and dark, not like in Arkansas."

It is true. Back in Arkansas we had a big house and big rooms, but nothing compared to this Galveston house.

"Well," I said more nicely, "what do you want me to do about it?"

"Can we sleep with you?" Samuel wondered, a star of light from my lamp reflecting off his dark eyes, making it look as though they brimmed with tears.

I gave in. They are sleeping by me right now, lightly snoring. I better turn out the light.

Before the crack of dawn the next day...

I forced myself to wake up this morning so I can write about the way the house looks before we leave. It may take me a while to describe the house, but well, let me just get started.

There are twelve rooms in all—six bedrooms (four upstairs), two bathrooms (one upstairs), a kitchen, a dining room, and two parlors (one upstairs). Oh, yeah, and an attic. So I guess thirteen.

Each bedroom has a luxurious bed. It must be a king size bed with pillows filled with a million goose feathers (or chicken feathers. I don't know. Some type of feathers). Several of the beds (like mine) have a canopy. The curtains of my canopy are green, while the rest of my room is painted a chocolate brown. Nathan, Anthony, Samuel, and I sleep upstairs (of course, the boys sleep in the same bed). Papa, Mother, and Edward sleep downstairs. The extra bedroom is for *guests only*.

Most of the bedrooms have paintings of children playing, while one has a beautiful young lady sitting in a chair and glancing out the window (I get that picture, lucky me!). Rugs sit on dark, glossy wood, their patterns showing where each one had been made from. Paris, Spain, China. My bedroom—along with Papa and Mother's, Edward's and the guest's—have a desk to write on, which I am writing on right now as Anthony and Samuel snooze away in my bed.

The kitchen is huge, with hundreds of cabinets (at least it seems) filled with tea cups, kettles, pans, pots, plates, forks, spoons, and knifes. Each plate has little blue flowers around the edge, while the tea cups have vines growing up the handles. There is a stove, an ice box, a fireplace, and even a cellar below the floorboards.

The dining room has fourteen seats (which probably makes you think the table is really long, because it is). Two chandeliers suspend from the ceiling, while more paintings hang from the walls, the talent of the artists showing off.

But the rooms I like the best are the parlors. There are so many instruments in that room. Papa's violin hangs from the wall, and there is also a piano and a harp. Grandma Ann gave that harp to Mother before she left Massachusetts, and although no one knows how to play it (Nathan is trying) we still must keep it. I don't complain about the large harp like Edward does because I think it is beautiful, with its delicate strings and golden neck.

There are two or three sofas in each parlor and a fireplace in the downstairs one.

Oh, the house is so beautiful. Wires run through the walls so we can have running water and electricity. I remember how large I thought our house was in Arkansas, and how small it seems now that we have this new house to compare it to. We had few friends, there in the town of Little Rock, though I don't quite know why. People just never seemed to be too keen with us. Maybe it was because we were some of the richest folks there, and, though I don't want to call it this, we seemed rather snobbish to them. I hope I am not really a snob. I stayed home mostly, except for school and playing with Kate. I scarcely miss Arkansas, and I am glad we are here in Galveston, where we can start over and maybe have more friends here than we did before. I would certainly love to have more than one friend

Great! Now my brothers know about my diary. Samuel had climbed out of bed and was hovering over my shoulder. He asked, "Where did you get that book, Emmie?" I jumped at the sound of his voice.

I almost answered until Anthony awoke. "What are you doing, Curt?" he asked, using Samuel's nickname.

"Emmie has a writing book, Herby."

As quick as a wink Anthony had bound out of bed and snatched the book from me. He began reading what I had written so far. "Before the c-crack of d-d-d—" I grabbed the book out of his hands.

"It's *dawn*," I said, hiding the book behind my back so he could not take it again.

"Where did you get that?"

"The attic."

"You did not."

"Yes I did," I insisted. "You would have found it instead of me if you wouldn't have been fiddling with your stupid rabbits."

"I'm telling Mother!" Anthony yelled, running towards the door and hurdling down the steps, Samuel behind him and me behind Samuel. It sounded as though a stampede of wild animals was coming through the house.

All three of us barged into our parent's room without knocking. Papa was buttoning his shirt, while Mother was fixing her hair. Both of them asked, at the same time, "What on earth is going on?"

Anthony and Samuel chattered like chipmunks how I had found a "secret writing book" that "was supposed to be" theirs when I "stole it."

"I did not steal it!"

Papa held up his hands to quiet everyone. The only noise to be heard was Nathan's cane thumping on the ground because he was walking down the steps. Edward was probably still sleeping because he can sleep through anything.

"Emelise," Papa said, "is that your book?"

"Yes, Papa."

"Well there you go boys. It's Emelise's book. No more arguing."

"But, Papa!" they exclaimed.

"Enough," he insisted. I smirked at the boys. Anthony stuck out his tongue.

"With all the noise you three were making," said Nathan as he stood in the doorway, that handsome smile of his radiating off the room and making everyone else grin as well, "you probably woke up the whole neighborhood. Maybe we could walk around town right now. Just go out in our pajamas and tell everyone elephants had not escaped from Africa and it was the noisy Carson family."

Mother rolled her eyes. "Oh, Nathan, really. But since we are up, why don't you, Emelise, help me with breakfast. Then we can go watch the town wake up."

"Yahoo!" Anthony shouted, forgetting all about my "secret writing book." "We're going to town!" Samuel and Anthony ran out of the room. I heard the door open and close as they stepped outside, ranting to the whole neighborhood about going to town for the first time since the move.

Mother hurried out of the room and opened the door. "Anthony! Samuel! Get in here and get changed."

After a delicious breakfast of ham and eggs...

Reading over what I had written, I realized I did not write about the outside of the house. There are two balconies. One is outside Nathan's bedroom, and the other is outside my bedroom. I like to go sit on the balcony and read. When we moved here the boys argued that they wanted a balcony, and why should Nathan when he couldn't even see? I thought that was rude and said they should apologize to Nathan. But kind, goodhearted Nathan only laughed and said, "They're right, you know. Why should I have a balcony? You boys can have my room if it makes you happy." Only Mother heard and marched into the conversation, saying she didn't want her two babies falling off the balcony and cracking their heads open on the ground below. "So, no."

There is also a white fence around the little yard and an apple tree, though it is barely large enough to produce proper apples.

So now you know what my house looks like, dear diary. It is painted white with red trim. Samuel likes to say it is the "Carson Candy Cane House."

We will be leaving soon. It took me ten minutes to figure out what I should wear. I finally decided on the green dress, my hair put up in a braided bun with a green bow, and lacy gloves. Everyone else is in their very best.

A driver is going to pick us up. Papa arranged everything. The driver will take us around town in a beautiful wagon and by lunchtime we will have seen most of the town. I hope we get to eat at a restaurant.

Around 4 o'clock...

What a day! Where to begin? There is so much to tell! Mother, Anthony, and Samuel are napping, while Edward, Nathan and Papa are sitting outside talking. I will not be bothered.

We did indeed eat at a restaurant, but I am getting ahead of myself.

Once our driver arrived—a tall and skinny driver—we piled into the carriage and began our long drive around the town of Galveston, Texas. Unluckily, I was sandwiched between the boys until Anthony decided he wanted to sit by

Samuel and climbed over me to get to him. He left a mark on my dress from his shoe. Boy, was I mad and almost shouted at him until Nathan, now next to me, gently touched my arm and shook his head. "It's good that you're by me, Emelise. Describe the scenery. Are the houses like ours? Big and fancy like?"

And so I told him. Houses as big as ours were lined along the road. Trees were planted into the ground right by the sidewalk. People paraded the streets, occasionally glancing through the shop windows. Numerous horses, tied against telephone poles and hooked to a carriage, shook their heads in protest, wanting to start the day and get moving.

Mother was hysterical when she saw the Tremont Opera House on 23rd Street, Avenue D. Mother loves opera, and can't stay away from shows. I didn't think it looked that grand, actually. The building reached four stories, and people crowded around the door so much they stood on the streets, but I thought it looked like the cotton mills we had seen before (of course I did not tell Mother this or she would have made me come with her to an opera show and I *hate* opera).

When we came to Avenue D, we saw St. Mary's Infirmary. It was three stories high with a white picket fence around the perimeter and naked trees trying to bear leaves.

26th Street had businesses and utility poles and many more people awaking from their slumber and ready to begin the Saturday morning.

We passed schools that were five times the size of houses. I even saw a negro school! It said on the sign, "Negro School." Right there on 26th Street. Negros seem to live here in Galveston more than in Little Rock—that I noticed.

Our driver remained silent throughout the entire trip, not saying one word. Maybe that is what drivers are supposed to be like, only taking us place to place and pretending to be mute.

Anthony and Samuel were so excited that they practically jumped out of the wagon and ran into the street, but I grabbed their shirts just in time. I could not blame them, really. I wanted to walk around just as much as they did, but we wanted to see *all* of Galveston did we not? Strolling would take forever.

I could not even believe how tall the buildings were! I tried to describe them to Nathan, but he seemed to understand I could find no words for the giant things—two, three, some even four stories high.

There were so many churches! Presbyterian, Baptist, Catholic, Protestant, Methodist Episcopal, and even some African American churches, though the sign didn't exactly say what religion the Africans had. Mother decided on the church we would be attending right when she saw it: St. Patrick's Catholic Church on 34th Street, Avenue J. Mother liked it because it was made out of brick and so huge. She wanted to walk inside (and probably say a rosary or two), but Papa convinced her that we could not stop and she would be in church tomorrow morning anyway. How she grumbled!

I still could not get over the houses, though. I thought *ours* was nice, being two stories and all, but I saw some that were four stories and had six balconies! One house had statues of lions by the marble staircase that led up to the gigantic door. Another had a pointed roof and it sort of resembled a castle. One house had palm trees planted in the yard! They were bigger than the house!

Throughout the trip my fears had increased. Will people here in Galveston consider me stuck-up and snobbish? Though those houses are grand, I did see some rather shabby looking ones. Will the poorer people gossip about us like they did in Arkansas? I dare hope not!

Getting back to the main event: There is so much to tell that I can hardly write fast enough! But now the most exciting part has come. I must describe every detail so I can remember later.

We went to *Ritter's Saloon & Restaurant* all the way over on Avenue B. Mother was not that thrilled when she read the *Saloon* part, but finally the driver piped up for the first time and said, "Ma'am, Ritter's has da best food in all of Galveston.

You don't gotta worry 'bout da Saloon part." Then he clammed up again. Anthony and Samuel began to giggle, until Edward slapped them hard, then they cried. I almost laughed as well. That man had to have had the strongest country voice I've ever heard! People here in Galveston talk a *little* strange, but this man! Ha! He had to have been from some other South place to have inherited such a hilarious tone. Papa smiled and nodded, saying thank you and telling the driver we would expect him back here in an hour.

Dinner was delicious. I had beef, corn, peas, potato slices (I *love* potatoes!) and chocolate cake for dessert.

Just as we were finishing up, a little girl—no older than six—came over to me. She had blond curls and wore a blue dress. "Hello," she said.

I glanced around, wondering where this little girl had come from. "Hello," I answered. "What is your name?"

"Esther."

"I'm Emelise. Where are your parents?"

She pointed to a table a few yards away from us. The man sitting there had a white beard and wore a white hat. He was dressed in a nice black suit. Noticing his daughter was gone, he spoke to his wife and two other daughters sitting there. They immediately pushed their chairs back and frantically looked around. The oldest daughter then spotted Esther and I saw the family sigh with relief.

They walked over to our table and the man introduced himself as Isaac Cline. "This is my wife, Cora." Cora had brown hair and was a few months pregnant. "You already met Esther, and my other two daughters are Allie May, age twelve, and Rosemary, eleven." Both the older girls had inherited their mother's fine, curly brown hair.

Papa introduced us, and Mr. Cline and he began chatting away. I heard enough to know that Mr. Cline is a meteorologist for the U.S Weather Bureau right here in Galveston, teaches Sunday school, was a professor at a local medical college, and earned his doctor of philosophy degree from AddRan Male &

Female College! Meteorologist Isaac Cline right before my very eyes! I had heard stories about him in the newspaper and how he is so famous here in Galveston, but to *meet* him was just unreal! (You are probably wondering, dear diary, how I can remember such complicated things, like where he got his doctor of philosophy degree, but, as I said before, I can remember certain things and forget the rest. Now that I think of it, I wonder if Mother gave me a chore to do before she went to take a nap. Oh, well. I will find out when she wakes up.)

The twelve year old, Allie May, stared at me as I stared at her father. She obviously wanted to talk with me, but I was so interested in the adult conversation I did not want to break away from the table and sit somewhere else with her. Of course, Mother saw me and spoke up. "Allie May, why don't you take Emelise with you to a different table and go chat? Emelise? Go along now."

"Do I have to?" I asked before I could stop myself. I knew it was the wrong thing to say the moment that question passed from my lips; it was just so rude.

"Emelise!" Mother snapped. "Go with Allie May while I talk with Cora."

"Yes, ma'am."

So I went with Allie May to a different table. It was very awkward, us just sitting there and wondering who would make the first move. But then she began chatting. I listened at first, until I realized she was one of those boring children who want to just sit and be sweet all day!

"Mama is expecting another baby," she said. "Everyone hopes it's a boy, that is, except Esther. She wants a sister. I'm not so sure I want another sister. I have two already. I want a brother this time."

"Why would you want a brother?" I asked, again, before I could stop myself. Where had my trademark shyness gone? There I was, blabbing away without even thinking of it.

Allie May cocked her head. "Why *wouldn't* you want a brother?"

"I have four, and three of them I wish were not my brothers."

The other girl went completely white. Her jaw dropped. Finally she managed, "Why would you say that?"

Luckily Papa and Mr. Cline the meteorologist called us over before I needed to answer. "Allie May, I hope you got to know this fine young lady Emelise a bit?"

Allie May glanced my way uncertainly, but nodded. "Yes, Papa."

"Good," the man said, satisfied. "Emelise's father and I had been talking, and we thought it is such a nice summer day that why don't we go to the beach for an hour or two?"

All the children—Esther, Rosemary, Samuel, and Anthony—
squealed with delight. Anthony began chatting with Rosemary about the time he went swimming at a freshwater pond and stepped on a sea urchin (this time I let him carry on with his folly instead of lecturing about where sea urchins *really* live). Samuel and Esther were giggling in a corner. I had never seen the boys apart before, so I was shocked when both of them were talking to girls.

Once outside the restaurant, we took separate carriages and drove through town, admiring the craftsmanship once more.

Soon we arrived at the beach. Papa said it was the Gulf of Mexico. I had always admired the large gulf in my history book, but I had never I thought I would actually play in its waters!

Everyone climbed out and took their shoes off. I offered to help Nathan to the water, but he smiled and said he could manage. Rosemary and Anthony, Esther and Samuel, were the first ones to get into the water. Anthony had been sticking by Rosemary for a time, and I couldn't help but think...no, Anthony is only eight, and Rosemary eleven. Not to mention Esther and Samuel being only six! I laughed to myself.

The water rushed over my feet as the sand squished

through my toes. It felt so good. Mother called to me, cautioning that I better not get my dress wet, but I didn't listen and ran into the water until it reached my knees.

After a while of playing, the adults decided the hottest part of the day was over and it was time to go home. I couldn't help but think of my sister right then and there. We had seen almost the whole town, but not the St. Mary's Orphan Asylum. Maybe Mother would not mind...

"Mother!" I called as she helped Cora into the wagon. "Can we go see Alice? I'm sure she can't be but half an hour away."

I saw Mother hesitate, and I knew she wanted to see her oldest child, but when she shook her head I knew my battle had been lost.

"Tomorrow afternoon will come soon enough, Emelise."

Nothing much happened after that. We drove home and the family went about their business (I love saying that).

Wait, I hear Anthony. He is waking up from his nap—the nap he refused to take and claimed he "wouldn't fall asleep no matter how much I try, so there's no point."

Now Mother calls. Papa, Edward, and Nathan are coming in the house from their talk on the porch. Edward didn't say one word the entire time we viewed Galveston. The only time he uncrossed his arms was when he hit the boys for laughing at our driver's voice. I wonder what is going on in that mind of his. Ruth Henry probably.

Later...

Thankfully, Mother did not instruct me to do a chore before she took her nap, so I was saved from being yelled at.

Nathan wanted me to help him with his Braille this evening. I am so proud of the way I have taught Nathan to read with his hands. I have a little bit of trouble with it myself, though. I can look at those dots and read right along, like a normal book, but there is no way I can close my eyes and place my hands on the book, reading the way Nathan does. It feels like sandpaper to me, and I don't know how he does it, even though *I* am the teacher and *he* is the student.

We went over our normal routine. I gave him a piece of paper and told him to write out the entire alphabet in Braille. This helps him remember where each dot goes. I checked his work, then he began reading aloud to me. Sometimes he is stuck and I must look to give him hints on what the words could be since he refuses to use the little vision he has and wants to read "as if I were completely blind." I always get sad when he says this. I know it is possible that Nathan could go entirely blind, but I refuse to believe it.

After Braille, Nathan *tries* to teach me how to play one of the instruments he can play. Today I chose the piano (I hate the horrible screeching sound the violin makes when I hit a wrong note, and Nathan hasn't quite mastered the harp yet). Nathan plays so beautifully. He composes his own songs and remembers them by heart (they are so beautiful, Mozart couldn't have done better himself). I don't know how he does it. I forget *everything* (everything I don't want to forget I forget, and everything I want to forget I don't forget) but semi-sightless Nathan remembers every single note.

I guess you can sort of guess how my lessons turned out: horrible. I hit wrong note after wrong note, and I swear I saw Nathan wince, even though he kept encouraging me and saying I was "getting along just fine with the piano."

I hear thunder now. It is going to rain. Anthony and Samuel just ran outside to make sure the rabbits "won't get wet."

Still later...

It is pouring! It sounds as though hail is pounding on the roof, though it is only large raindrops. Everything looks ghostly now. The few lamps lit in the parlor cast an eerie glow along the wall as the lightning brightens the room back up. Oh! A slight breeze is coming through the window, giving me goose-bumps. There. I just told Anthony to shut it. That's better.

Now Mother is fretting that the new flowers she planted will be ruined. Edward was sitting at the desk, writing a letter to you-know-who when Papa called him. The letter is still on the desk. I wonder what he wrote...

Be right back.

Here I am again. I snuck over to the desk and pretended to be organizing it when I was really reading the letter. Here is what he wrote (maybe not word for word, but that is as much as I could remember in such little time):

August 25, 1900
Dear Ruth,

Words can't express how much I miss you. Galveston is nowhere near as nice a place as Little Rock—mostly because you aren't here with me.

I have tried to change Father's mind about me going back to Little Rock when I finish college, but he still says no.

Do not worry, Ruth. I promise you, right here and now, I will come back to you very soon. I guarantee it.

I am worried about the *I will come back to you very soon*. What does he mean? Is he going to run away? I wouldn't mind to see Edward go, but *still*. He is my brother. Maybe I should tell someone.

Oh, no. Thunder just shook the house like a mythical giant trying to uproot us from the ground, which made me spill some ink on my skirt. Mother is going to be furious.

The thunder rattling the house seems to be getting louder, as if angry at me for looking at my brother's letter. But how could I not? It was almost as if Edward *wanted* me to read his letter, with him just leaving it out in the open. Or maybe the thunder is trying to persuade me to tell someone about the information I have unlocked. *Boom!* Louder each time. My heart is hammering. *Boom! Why did you look at your brother's private things? Boom! Tell someone about your findings! Boom!* Stop! Stop! Stop!

Sunday, August 26, 1900

I had trouble sleeping last night. The menacing thunder did not help sooth my conscience. I actually walked out of my room and into my parents and stood at the foot of their bed, rehearsing what I would say about the letter. But when thunder echoed through the house and lighting split the sky, I grew frightened and darted back to my room, hiding under the covers and praying morning would come soon.

And it has come. I will try to write happier thoughts. Alice will arrive at any moment and I don't want to have a gloomy face. (Oh, yeah. Instead of showing Mother my ink-blotted dress, I hid it under my bed. I hope to soak it or repair it somehow before she notices it missing.)

Everyone dressed in their very best once again. Papa had told our driver yesterday when to arrive, and he pulled up just in time. It was a beautiful day, and yesterday's rain made the flowers blossom and cleaned the streets.

St. Patrick's Catholic Church, right there on 34th Street, Avenue J, appeared even larger than when we had seen it yesterday. It was very long, with a large arc that we walked under to get inside. The whole thing had been constructed out of brick, and I thought it was very pretty with the sun shining on the faded red stones.

We took our seats right in the front row (Mother hates to sit in the back because "I can't see with peoples' heads in the way!"). There were many people, all reverently bowing their heads, their lips silently forming the words to the Our Father as the rosary they held clanked against the pews.

Mother nudged me when she saw me staring, and I quickly closed my eyes, trying to concentrate on the Glorious Mysteries, but couldn't. The church was so large and beautiful! Statues of Jesus scattered around the place, candles lit up the church, their glow turning the color of the glass that surrounded the flame, the colors from the stained glass windows reflected onto the floor.

Our priest came and the mass began. We sang hymns—everyone did, that is, except Edward. He pretended to sing but I heard nothing come out of his lips. Once again, I thought of the letter. Was he thinking of running away?

The homily was quite long, and I found it hard to pay attention. The priest kept pounding on the pulpit and shouting, his face growing red. I know Mother did not approve of that very much, but she would not change churches now that we had come to this one—one of her rules. To me, it seemed more like a Baptist Revival—the way the priest hammered on—than a nice, quiet, Catholic homily.

When Communion came, I had guilt on my conscience. Would I be sinning receiving Communion when I had read the private thoughts of my brother? I hoped not.

Anthony and Samuel were well behaved during mass, only laughing once because the priest had shouted so much that he started to cough until someone brought him a glass of water.

After that we went home, changed, and now I am waiting for Alice to get here. I know she is very busy over at the orphanage, but I wish she could come faster. I wish to see her (and I am also very hungry. Mother won't let us eat until she gets here).

Will my sister still be the same? Will she have the same frizzy hair and same small chin? Will she still be a good listener? Will she

Later...

Sorry to leave so abruptly like that, diary. My sister arrived!

Anthony and Samuel came running through the house, shouting, "Alice is here! Alice is here!" Sorry, diary, but I was so excited I tossed you on the floor and bolted to the door. There was Alice, right before my eyes strolling through the street. She wore the usual clothing a Sister would wear, something called a habit. She also had a head piece on, and it sort of looked like a wedding veil (except it was black and didn't cover her face, just her hair). I stood in the doorway for a moment as my sister walked on the sidewalk towards the house. For some reason, I felt shy. My sister *seemed* the same. It was hard to tell if she had frizzy hair because of the head piece, but everything else matched up to the young lady years before.

Soon Alice saw me. I don't know if it is a sin for a Sister to run, but Alice did so. She spread her arms out and jogged towards me. My shyness disappeared and I hugged my sister, the sister I had not seen for years. "Emelise, Emelise," she kept saying. "How I have missed you."

"I missed you too, Alice," I choked out. It sounded like such a weak sentence to say to someone whom you have not seen in years, but it was all I could think of. My sister's arms wrapped around me tightly and I didn't want her to let go. But soon the rest of the family came out: Papa, Mother, Edward, Nathan, Anthony, Samuel. Everyone climbed on top of each other (even Edward!) and hugged Alice until I was sure she would be flattened. Mother cried a river, blubbering, "My little baby has grown up." Papa smiled all the while, complimenting, "You have grown into a fine women, Alice. We're very proud." Edward and Nathan only grinned. Anthony kept saying, "Did you bring presents for us?" Samuel asked, "Yeah, presents?"

Somehow everyone was able to detach themselves from Alice and move into the house, where we all settled down at the dinner table, said grace, and began eating. Alice hardly ate anything because she had to answer questions!

"How many orphans are with you in the orphanage?"

"Ninety-three children, ten Sisters."

"Are they difficult to handle?"

"No, they are very sweet."

"Do you ever get time by yourself?"

"Well, the children always need help."

Anthony and Samuel asked again if she had brought them presents and Alice nodded. She reached down into her bag, pulling out two handkerchiefs—both red.

"We needed new ones!" Anthony exclaimed, grabbing Samuel's hand and running from the table to go tie them on.

I thought we were rushing everything a little bit. I mean, my sister just walked through the door—we haven't seen her in years—and we sat down and ate, asking her questions. She never got to ask *us* questions or look around the house or even freshen up! Maybe everyone was just excited. But finally, after lunch, I mentioned, "Maybe Alice would like to relax," and the family agreed they would be more comfortable in the parlor.

We sat down on the sofas. Alice still kept her head piece on. Maybe Sisters have to keep them on all the time, I don't know, but I wish she would take it off so I could see if she still had frizzy hair. Papa said, "Why don't we let Alice tell us how her life has been since moving to Galveston."

"Of course, Papa," she said. She sighed. "I have fallen in love with Galveston. It is a wonderful town, Papa. The people are so friendly, the buildings so magnificent, and the food in restaurants to extraordinary! I was lucky enough to go to one of the many restaurants when I first arrived here." My sister clasped her hands together. "Oh, I am so glad you have decided to come here! I know I will be going back to school soon, but I simply do not want to think about that day."

I did not want to think of that day either.

She continued, "The orphans are the sweetest children anyone can imagine. They have been through so much. We want to isolate the children from everyone else so they do not carry something contagious back to the orphanage which is why the orphanage is located away from town and by the beach. But they do not seem to mind living so far away from town. We are, as I mentioned, right next to the beach, and the children love to run and play in the water. Some of the Sisters oppose to them going anywhere near the ocean, but the salty air and playtime does them good." Alice clasped her hands together and sighed once more. "Oh, it is so beautiful by the beach. Every morning I wake up to rushing water crashing on the rocks and the sea gulls calling to each other. In evening, the sun sets over the never ending ocean and the sky is breathtaking. It looks as though someone is painting a master piece, blending pastels of all colors on the sky, just as if it were a wet canvas." My sister stared off into the distance, a hint of a smile forming on her lips. How I wished we lived by the beach! It sounded so serene and magnificent…

Alice said, "As I explained before, there are ninety-three children and ten Sisters. We have two dorms, one for the boys and one for the girls. The girls' is new and much stronger. We hope to make the boys' just as sturdy, but we don't have enough money right now. The Sisters are always worrying about money. It is not easy to take care of ninety children plus ourselves."

"I would think so!" Mother exclaimed.

Alice nodded, continuing her story. "Sister Elizabeth Ryan is usually the one who goes to town. The rest of us hardly ever leave the orphanage for fear of carrying a contagious disease. I almost had to beg the Sisters to let me come visit you, and they only allowed me to if I had prayed to Sweet Jesus before, asking him to spare the children from a sickness."

"Tell us about the children," Nathan insisted.

"All right," Alice said, smiling. "We just had a boy and his brother come in not too long ago—William Murney, his name is. He is a sweet thirteen year old boy. Their mother died of tuberculosis and the father of a heart attack the next day. William takes care of his little brother splendidly. They hardly leave each others side. They are all they have left."

"The poor dears," Mother mentioned.

"Yes," Alice agreed. "The little boy is quiet, being only eight and losing both of his parents, but William is very strong. I would like to have such courage."

Mother changed the subject. "Has anything bad ever happened to the children other than the yellow fever?"

"Yes. Other than the yellow fever, there was a fire in 1875, then a severe hurricane storm damaged the girls' dorm, which is why the new one was built." Alice's faced turned from a happy one from telling stories of William Murney and his brother, to a grim one, her face even losing color.

"A hurricane?!" Mother exclaimed. "Here? In Galveston? How bad?"

Alice fingered the crucifix hung around her neck. "Bad, Mother."

"But can't it happen again? How do we know a hurricane isn't going to ruin Galveston tomorrow?"

"A meteorologist here in Galveston—Isaac Cline, I believe his name is—said—"

"Wait, you mean the Mr. Cline we met yesterday?" I asked.

"Did you meet him yesterday, Emelise, dear?" Alice asked. "His wife's name is Cora, I think, and he has three daughters..."

"That's him! We met him!"

"Shush, Emelise," Edward snapped. I knew he was careful not to tell me to shut up like he had done once before.

I glared at my brother, but let Alice continue.

"Some years ago, the Sisters say, Mr. Cline wrote in the Galveston *News* that the thought of a hurricane ever doing any serious harm to Galveston was *a crazy idea*. Some of the people in Galveston disagreed with him and wanted a seawall built, but most think, because he is a meteorologist, he knows what it best. You don't have to worry, Mother."

"Thank goodness we can trust Mr. Cline," Papa said.

"Amen," Alice whispered.

After a moment of silence, Alice asked us to tell her about our trip from Little Rock and so forth. Everyone took turns. Anthony kept cutting in and saying how the rabbits enjoyed the train ride, then he told her, "You never saw them! They've missed you!"

Alice smiled and said, "I'll come out and see them in a little while, honey."

Anthony protested. "But they miss you *now*. I'll go get one. Curt, come with me." They scurried off.

Soon they came back. Anthony had a white rabbit with brown ears cradled in his arms. The rabbit's nose twitched and it started to kick its legs, wanting to be let down. Samuel was right behind his brother, a rabbit in his arms.

"Fluffy! Stop! Alice is here."

My sister gently took the kicking rabbit out of Anthony's arms and began stroking it. White fur stuck to her dress, and I wondered what the Sisters at the orphanage would think when Alice came back with fur all over her.

"This is Fluffy?" she asked. "How big he has grown! You have taken wonderful care of your rabbits, Anthony." My brother puffed up his chest with pride.

"What about me?" Samuel asked, placing his rabbit in her lap as well. "Doesn't Freddy look nice, too?"

"Oh, yes, he does."

Only then did Mother seem to notice the rabbits sitting practically on her sofa. She stood up and ordered to get those "filthy creatures" out of her house.

Anthony protested. "But, Mother, they aren't filthy! Curt and I just cleaned their cage *and* them before Alice came. They are cleaner than the house."

"Get them out!"

The two boys grumbled, but took the rabbits off Alice's lap and marched outside.

After another hour or two of chatting, Alice said, "I better be heading back to the orphanage. The Sisters will need me to help with supper soon, and it is a long way to the Sandy Beach."

"Let me drive you," Papa offered, standing.

Alice shook her head. "Thank you, Papa, but no. I am already breaking one of their usual laws by coming here. I don't want you to come to the orphanage and give them a fright about diseases. They can send me back to the school early, you know."

"Of course."

"But can't we see the orphans *some* time?" I asked. I dearly wanted to meet William Murney and his brother. Maybe William could use a friend just as much as I needed one. I know there are so many children at the orphanage that he probably has ninety friends, but maybe...

"I don't know..." Alice questioned. I knew she wanted me to come to the orphanage with her, but the Sisters were so afraid. "I will ask the Sisters. Maybe they can allow one child to come."

"If you don't mind," Nathan butted in, "I would like to come as well."

"All right, two children. I will ask, Emelise. Don't worry."

We called goodbye as Alice walked down the street towards Sandy Beach. She turned and waved, and I saw white fur stuck to the front of her black dress. I laughed.

Monday, August 27, 1900

This is why I hate my brother's rabbits so much! I wish they would run away for good! After such a good day yesterday, this!

Let me start over before I get so angry I break my pencil. Then I will have to sharpen it and that will take forever so let me just calm down. Right before breakfast Anthony and Samuel went out to feed the rabbits. A few moments later they came barging in, literally screaming loud enough to shake the roof down, "The rabbits are gone! All three of them! We must find them!"

Everyone groaned so loud, especially me. Edward grabbed a sausage link right out of the frying pan and said he was "too busy" to help. So much for that big brother. Mother claimed she wouldn't help, and Papa had business in town to tend to, though now that I think of it, *what* business did he have? We just moved here and he had *business*?! Sure! Nathan volunteered to help, but Anthony just rolled his eyes and looked at me, as if to say, "You helped us catch them in Little Rock, you got to help us catch them here in Galveston, too."

"No!" I said, but Mother wheeled around and told me to

help them "this instant."

"She doesn't have to, Mother," dear, sweet Nathan said. "I will help the boys."

Mother smiled. "I know you mean well, Nathan, but there really isn't anything you can do to help catch those quick rabbits. Why don't you set the table?"

I saw the disappointment in my brother's face. It **is those** types of days that I can tell he wishes he could see. But obedient Nathan went to set the table without a second thought. Why can't I be more like him? But as dogged as I am, I claimed I would not help them. "They're their rabbits, they can catch them."

Anthony immediately started to wail, which sent a chain reaction right to Samuel, and he started crying as well. "We'll never see Fluffy or Freddy or Fuzzy again!" (I don't know what is with the *F's*, so don't ask.)

Mother set her hands on her hips, like she does when she is angry, and pointed towards the door. "You go right out that door, Miss Emelise Carson, and catch those rabbits. If you don't, I will not allow you to go to the orphanage with Alice." I wanted to tell Mother that Alice hadn't even said yes to the orphanage-coming-along question, but I held my tongue. It was bad enough to have to catch those stupid rabbits, but to not go to the orphanage, if granted, would ruin the whole week.

"Fine," I grumbled, stomping out the door, the boys, all of the sudden dry-eyed and cheery, skipping behind me. The last thing I saw when I closed the door was Nathan giving me a sympathetic look.

"All right," I then said. "Show me the hut." The boys led the way to the rabbit hut. Papa had constructed it three feet off the ground, with the house two feet off the ground. There was a ladder that led up to it, and numerous toys scattered about the run around area.

"Here," A pointed. "I hadn't forgotten to shut the door like before"—I rolled my eyes. There had certainly been a before—"but instead, the cage is torn open."

I bent down and examined the damage. The rabbits had not chewed through the wire, that was clear, because the hole was far too large for them to create in only one night. Besides, it looked as though the cage had been pulled on and torn from the pressure. I wondered what had happened.

S grabbed my arm. "Look!" I turned towards the road and what did I see trying to hop across? One of the rabbits—Fluffy, Freddy, Fuzzy, whoever. The rabbit's ears were up, and I could see him gingerly taking a step forward, only a wagon came and almost trampled him.

"Go get him, Emelise!" A squealed.

I sighed. Why did I have to be the one? Hurrying over to the road, I mumbled under my breath about eating those stupid things. How many times had they escaped? And what good did they do anyway? We couldn't eat them—well, we *could,* but the boys didn't want to. They don't give us milk like a cow, or wool like a sheep. They didn't snuggle up by you like a cat, or play fetch like a dog. What *do* they do, I would like to know?

Luckily, this one didn't give me too much trouble. I walked to the opposite side of the road and ran towards it (watching for oncoming traffic, of course). The rabbit practically jumped out of its skin and ran back in the yard, into the hut, going through the hole it had come out of. One down, two to go.

I knew from experience that the last two rabbits were the rascals. They were the ones who probably planned every escape plan, every runaway. I hated catching them. How many times have I mentioned that, I wonder? Well, I do. Even worse, our house was right in front of the street...and it was a beautiful day. People awoke from their sleep and went outside to sit on their porches and read the morning paper. Except, I knew far too well that they were not actually reading the paper—they were watching me catch a white ball of fluff that zig-zagged across the yard.

"There he is!' A and S would shriek. "Catch him! Catch

him!"

"You know," I panted, "this would be a whole lot easier if you two would *help* me."

"We can't," A said. "Curt and I are watching this rabbit so it doesn't get away." Of course.

After hours of trying to catch those rabbits and having them almost head into the street, I had caught the second one. Two for three. By that time, I was hungry, sweating, and positively boiling in anger. Edward had actually come out of the house and sat on the porch, watching us—me really—run around. When I snagged my dress on Mother's thorn bush, he burst out laughing. "Shut *up*!" I said, shocked at my words. I sounded like Edward! Mother rushed out of the house and told me if she ever heard me say that again I would get my mouth washed out with soap. Edward smirked. How come she can catch *me* saying that, but never Edward?

Nathan came out later, too. He tried to listen for the rabbits, or anything he thought would be helpful, but he didn't contribute to the cause at all. "I hear something over there," he would say. But when I looked the rabbit I had cornered before ran as soon as my eyes were taken from it.

Finally, when everyone else had eaten lunch—*including* A and S, might I add—the last rabbit had itself in a pickle. There I was, on my stomach under the filthy porch. Yes! Under the porch! The rabbit had squeezed through the white fencing surrounding the porch and hidden in the way back. I can't write down how many spiders crawled on me or how many times my hair got caught on a nail. My knees were bleeding—torn at the stockings—and I felt disgusting.

The rabbit—Fluffy, A claimed it was, though I don't know how he can tell the difference between the three— cowered on the corner, panting. I reached out and tried to grab it. A had instructed me not to grab it by the ears or neck. Right now I didn't care if I grabbed it by the tail and yanked it off. I was *going* to catch the rabbit—now—or the boys would have to either get it themselves or live with two.

As quick as lightning, I grabbed a tuft of fur and pulled the animal towards me, cradling it. Only then it started to kick. My arms got scratched and started to bleed. I almost dropped it, but I managed to hold it tightly in an embrace. I crawled out of the porch and handed it to the boys. They thanked me over and over, saying the rabbits would be extra nice to me, but I really didn't care at all. I went in the house and took a bath. Might I add that the water turned slightly brown from all the dirt I had collected?

When I finished and went downstairs, the boys were telling a rather *different* tale to Mother.

"And it ran on the road, and I caught and brought it back to the hut! Then the last one was under the porch and I grabbed it and pulled it to safety!"

"How brave of you," Mother complimented. "Maybe you should take a bath?"

"Oh, no," A said, shaking his head. "Curt and I aren't dirty one bit, are we, Curt?"

"Nope," S agreed. "Not one bit, Herby."

Mother smiled. "All right then. Go play with the rabbits and make sure they don't escape again."

"Yes, ma'am!"

Next Day…

Where is Alice? It has been almost forty-eight hours since her visit. Surely it does not take forty-eight hours to ask the Sisters of the orphanage if a teenage girl and her brother may tour the place. I think I will die of waiting.

I'll see if the mail has arrived. Maybe there is something for me.

Two minutes later...

Can I foresee the future? A letter came from Kate! I will paste it here or else someone in my family will end up throwing it away.

> *August 5, 1900*
> *Dearest Em,*
>
> *Sorry if this letter arrives later than it is supposed to. I had it sealed and ready to go the minute you left for your new home, but it lay on my bureau for days, untouched. I finally remembered and mailed it.*
>   *Please write me every little detail on how glorious Galveston looks. You are lucky. Papa insists we stay here in Little Rock. Maybe if he didn't own the Mercantile we would move more.*
>   *However, I do have some good news, though I have been melancholy since your departure. Do you remember Jordan Hanes from down the road? I think he has eyes for me. During church service he continued to turn his head and glance my way. When I smiled, he blushed. I don't really mind that he has eyes for me, since he is rather handsome, if you recall.*
>   *Well, I must go. Mama is going to need me to help with* something.
>
>   *Your forever friend,*
>
>   *Kate*

Isn't that like Kate to mention boys in her letters? That is all she thinks about everyday all the time. And about the "I have been melancholy since your departure" part, I don't mean to talk bad about my friend, but Kate is *never* melancholy, even if the worst disaster of them all happens. She is forever happy and as busy as a squirrel, not to mention just as chattery.

I will write her back.

Later...

Mother suggested, "Why don't you make some apple dumplings? You are so good with the recipe Grandmother Carson gave you." At first I was quite shocked. Mother never complimented me on anything, and if she did, she usually had a negative edge to her tone. This time, there was no disapproval. I hurried to the kitchen and began cooking. I will paste the recipe here. Grandmother gave it—along with a silver locket—to me minutes before she died when I was eleven years old. I know the spelling is not the greatest, and I was thinking of erasing it, but it is my grandmother's own penmanship and I don't want to change it. Grandmother wasn't always proud of her writing, so she hardly picked up a pencil, except for writing down recipes.

No, I mustn't cry. I do miss my grandmother horribly. We did almost everything together, from reading to baking, to walking to talking. I was closer to her than I am my own best friend.

The apple dumplin' recipe of Cynthia Lorraine Carson

1 1/2 cups suger
2 cups water
1/2 tsp. ground cinamon

1/2 tsp. ground nutmeg
1/4 cups margerine
2/3 cups suger
2 homemade pie crusts (see my other recipe)
8 good-looking apples, peeled and cored
3 tbsp. margerine, cut in slices

1. Boil 1 1/2 cups suger, 2 cups water, 1/4 tsp. cinamon, and 1/4 tsp. nutmeg to boil over the stove. Stir. Remove. Stir in 1/4 cups of margerine.
2. Add the other 2/3 cups suger, and 1/4 tsp. cinamon, and 1/4 tsp. of nutmeg.
3. Cut homemade pie crusts in half and roll in 8 inch circels. Put 1 apple in center of each circel. Sprinkel suger on top. Dot 3 tbsps. margerine evenly.
4. Fold doe over apples, pinching it to seel. Place in a pan. Pour seerup on top. Bake till golden brown.

    While I had been baking (the dumplings are in the oven now) Anthony and Samuel came marching over, asking me what I was doing.

    "Making apple dumplings."

    "Granny's recipe?" Anthony wondered.

    "Yes." They squealed with delight.

    "Can we have some now?" Samuel asked quietly.

    I shook my head. "They aren't done yet. I'm still boiling the ingredients."

    "Please, Emelise?" Anthony wailed. "Just an apple slice?"

    "No," I answered firmly and shooed them away. They did leave, but not before both of them stuck their hands in the sugar jar and ran away with a handful. White snow sprinkled on the floor.

    Nathan came in while I was sweeping the floor.

    "Apple dumplings, I presume?"

I sighed, but grinned. "Yes."

"And let me guess, Anthony and Samuel snitched some sugar."

"How'd you know?"

Nathan laughed and walked to the sink. I am continuously amazed the way he can walk around the house without running into something, but then again, he can see objects.

Nathan grabbed a rag, soaked it in water, walked back to me, knelt down, and began helping. "So I'm right?"

"Yes," I nodded.

"No wonder. I heard them running by, snickering something about how good they fooled you. Anthony led the robbery, didn't he?"

"I swear, it is Anthony who teaches Samuel those bad manners. Why can't that boy leave Samuel alone and not pass down his mischievousness?"

Nathan smiled. "They are boys, Emelise. Let them have a little fun." This time, Nathan sounded too much like Mother. I didn't like it.

I smell the apple dumplings. Better check to see if they are done.

Bedtime...

The apple dumplings were delicious, and everyone had seconds (except Edward; he had thirds and tried to hide his pleasure, but I know no one can resist Grandmother Carson's apple dumplings).

Tuesday, August 28, 2013

So here I am, sitting on the sofa writing while the older family members are huffing and puffing, trying to calm down after what happened this evening.

Papa and Edward argued. This is the first time they have since the move.

Everyone had almost finished their supper when Papa announced he had a surprise for Edward. Edward narrowed his eyes, gritted his teeth, and stared at his plate. Apparently, Papa's idea of a *surprise* is not the same as Edward's.

"Ah-hem," my father cleared his throat. "I happened to run into someone important today."

"The president?" Anthony questioned, eager as ever.

Papa laughed. "Good guess, but no. Anyone else want to try?"

When no one said anything, Papa proudly said he had met the principle of a university here in Galveston. "I told him about how bright Edward is and how he is getting ready to go to college. Then the man suggested why doesn't Edward go to *his* university? He said he will have no trouble getting Edward in. He may have to take a few tests to see if he can qualify, but as smart as Edward is he should have no trouble."

I wanted to laugh. Edward? Bright? But I didn't. Everyone else—except Anthony and Samuel, who gave no care and just enjoyed their chocolate pudding—was shocked and sullen.

"When were you going to discuss this with me, James?" Mother asked, fingering her necklace like she does when she is nervous or worried.

Papa seemed as taken-aback as everyone else, except his reason was different. "I am discussing it now, Lillian. You know, I figured you would be kind of excited at this opportunity for our son."

Mother came to reason now. She stood up and clasped

her hands together. "Of course! Edward, we are so proud of you. You have come a long way." She turned to Papa. "When can he take the tests?" And there they went, chatting about when would be a good time for Edward to go to the university and look around.

"What do you think, son?" Papa asked. But his smile faded when he saw Edward clutch his napkin fiercely.

"So you just decided all this without me saying anything?" Edward asked coldly.

"Say what you want now, Edward," Papa stated. "But this is a wonderful opportunity for you and it may not come again. Think of your future!"

Edward stood up so briskly he knocked over his chair, frightening the boys. They ran to Mother and stood behind her. Nathan looked down at his lap. I tried not to smile. Sometimes, though it may not be very nice of me, I like it when Edward gets something he doesn't want.

"I *am* thinking of my future!" he bellowed. "I have been thinking of my future for the past two years!"

"Edward," Papa said more calmly, "you know what I have told you about Ruth Henry. She is a sweet girl, but neither you nor she is ready to get married at such a young age. And besides, with this new information, you should be turning your attention to a *better* future."

My brother blew up with rage. He does get angry so easily, but I guess I understand. He loves Ruth Henry, and she loves him (though I don't know why, since he isn't handsome). I would just hate it if I thought I had my future all planned out and someone came and told me it was going to be different.

"You never think of me! Just because you earned a degree in college doesn't mean I have to! It isn't what I want!"

"I understand that—"

"No, you don't! Even though I am your son, you don't understand me." Then he broke the information that I have been holding inside of me since the Saturday I read his letter. "I am not staying here. I hate it here. As soon as I have enough money and find a way to get there, I am going back to Little Rock and *never* coming back."

Papa was so shocked at Edward's words that he tumbled backwards a few steps. Mother gasped, stood, and ran out of the room. Nathan remained mute, but I sighed with relief. The secret was finally out in the open.

When Edward ran outside, Papa followed, shouting that the conversation had not ended and they still needed to talk.

Of course, since the adults left and the boys would not help, Nathan and I had to clear the table. We remained quiet throughout the whole time, and then I went and got my diary to write this down while it is fresh.

I really don't know what to think. What would be worse, Edward leaving to a university here and Galveston where he can still visit and torment me because he is so angry, or him permanently heading back to Little Rock? I mean, even though he isn't the sweetest peppermint stick in the jar, he is still my brother…

Next Day…

Edward is not here! He never returned last night. Just stomped out of the house and left, nary a word about where he was going or when he would be back. I am going to find out where he went by wondering around town today (without Mother's knowledge, of course. She would just tell me to stay home and dust something of hers).

There has still been no word from Alice about me going to the orphanage.

Evening the same day...

Well, I asked around town if anyone has seen a tall, brown haired young man, but everyone I questioned only laughed at me and turned back to their work. I guess it is sort of silly. There could be hundreds of tall, brown haired young men in Galveston!

But I do have some interesting news. I saw Mr. Cline again, walking with little Esther. Esther was holding her father's hand and skipping over the cracks in the sidewalk, chanting the nursery rhyme, "Twinkle, Twinkle, Little Star."

Mr. Cline caught sight of me. "Emelise!" he called. "Good to see you again. How are your parents?"

I curtsied. "Very well, thank you." (It wasn't a lie; they *were* not sick, only angry.) "I hope your wife is the same?"

Mr. Cline was pleased at my courteous manners, I could tell. Maybe all those lessons back in Little Rock at Ms. Sinclair's Private School for Young Ladies did me good.

The older man said, "She is doing very well, thank you."

Esther spoke. "I miss Sam. When can I see him?"

Mr. Cline laughed a good hearty laugh, one that made anyone near him laugh, too. I thought of what Alice had said about Mr. Cline calling a gigantic hurricane ruining Galveston a crazy idea, and how he did not want to put up a seawall. Though that rumination was written three years ago, I wondered if Mr. Cline still considered his opinion one of certainty. I couldn't help but ask, ignoring Esther's question completely now that those new view points had entered my mind.

Again, Mr. Cline laughed. "You are a smart and curious girl Emelise. I appreciate your questions. I believe there is no need to worry whatsoever about a large hurricane coming to Galveston." He sighed. "But since there had been a few small ones these past few years, I am sorry to say not all the citizens of this town agree with my notion. Nonetheless, there is no need to worry. You just moved here, Emelise! Have a good time. Did you happen to notice the Tremont Opera House while you were touring the town? I have been there numerous times myself and I highly recommend getting tickets for this Saturday night."

Ugh! Opera! How I hate it! But of course I couldn't say, "No, Mr. Cline, no way am I going there because I hate opera." So instead I smiled and told him how Mother adored opera and I would notify her about his idea.

"All right then. Splendid. Esther and I better be going. Say bye, darling."

"Bye, Emmie!" Esther waved. "Tell Sam I said hello and that I miss him."

Right as they were heading off, I remembered my manners once more and invited Mr. Cline to Sunday dinner. He accepted! Oh, I am excited. A famous meteorologist coming for dinner! Edward better be home and better be in a good mood.

Thursday, August 30, 1900

Edward is home. Boy, was Papa mad when his oldest son walked through the door this morning, not giving the slightest indication of where he had been all day yesterday. I wonder where he *has* been. He had to have slept in a hotel of some sort, since he was gone two nights. I think I will go ask him. He will probably just tell me to shut up and order me out of his room, but what do I have to lose?

Five minutes later...

Dear diary, what did I tell you? I knocked, he opened, and then slammed the door in my face. At least he didn't snap at me. His face was grim and angry—like always—and his room was messy—like always. But one peculiar thing that I noticed when he shut the door was the smell. It smelled like the ocean and fish. Had he been fishing? All yesterday? Oh, this is like a regular mystery from the books!

Friday, August 31, 2013

Where is Alice????? It has been five days since her visit and no word, not even a telegram that the Sisters were still deciding! I don't even know if she has asked them yet.

    I am still thinking of William M. and his brother. The poor things (I sound like Mother!). I hope to become good friends with him. IF ONLY ALICE WOULD SEND WORD!!

Later...

Thank Heaven for neighbors. The rabbits almost escaped again! And now I know how they got out the first time.

    Our neighbor, Mrs. Sealy who lives in a gigantic house with a huge balcony, just happened to be sitting on the porch when she heard a commotion of some sort coming from our yard (she told us this later). Curious, she walked over and what did she see? A dog! A mangy cur was growling at the rabbits and scratching on the wiring, trying to get its paws all over those fuzz balls. Mrs. Sealy hurried to our door—as fast as a descent lady with manners can hurry—and summoned us outside. "Mrs. Carson, there's a crazy dog in your yard!" she shrieked.

Anthony, Samuel, and I bolted around the side and came face to face with the ugliest dog in the world. I guess he used to be white, but now was a lighter brown. He was small, but furious and continued to scratch on the rabbit wiring. Samuel started to cry, blubbering, "Get him, Emelise! Freddy and Fuzzy and Fluffy are going to get eaten!" Me *again*? I turned to Papa, and he marched over to the dog, grabbed the fur on its neck, and carried it away. I was surprised the dog did not try to bite Papa, but he only whimpered.

Anthony and Samuel were overjoyed the rabbits were okay. A said, "Told you, Emmie! Told you it was not out fault they got out." Boy, do I hate it when they are right.

Mama thanked Mrs. Sealy immensely. The lady only nodded and said she was glad to help.

I am not sure what Papa did with that dog. Maybe there is an animal shelter somewhere in Galveston that'll take him, even if he is as ugly as anything I have ever seen.

Saturday, September 1, 2013

Finally! Finally! Finally! Alice sent word! And as you can tell, dear diary, it is good news.

A messenger came to the door this morning just as we sat down for breakfast. Mother mumbled about the "indecency" of those people and they couldn't even let her eat her breakfast could they?

"It's for you," Mother told me, handing me the small envelope marked, "Emelise Carson of Galveston, Texas, 23rd Street."

Here is what my sweet sister wrote:

Dearest Emelise,

I am so sorry for the delay of this letter. I know you must have been anxiously awaiting an answer from the Sisters.
    They did not approve of you and Nathan coming at first, and it took days for me to convince them. It was all the more difficult when one of the little girls grew ill a day after I returned. They were terribly scared that I had carried something contagious back to the orphanage. Luckily, she only had a bad cold and nothing more.
    After reverently praying to Sweet Jesus in hopes of a yes from them, Sister Elizabeth came to me and said the Sisters have agreed to let you and Nathan come and visit the orphanage Monday afternoon. Papa may take you to Sandy Beach, but he must not come in, if you wish to respect the requests of the Sisters.
    I will see you Monday, my dear sister. The children are restlessly counting down the days; I think your visit is just what they needed to brighten their spirits.
                        Your forever sister,
                            Alice E. Carson

    YES! I am so happy. Finally I can go to the orphanage. And tomorrow Mr. Cline comes! Two exciting events in such a short period of time! Even better, Nathan gets to come! He is just as excited as I am. Oh, I will get to meet William Murney and his little brother and all the other children and maybe we could play on the beach! I better put this pen away, for I am blotching up the paper.

P.S—I completely forgot about the ink stained dress under my bed until now. But I am too busy to mend it now. Some other time.

After going to the store with Mother...

Mother bought the most horrid garment at the general store! I *never* want to be a lady after seeing that. I think I may run away from home if she forces me to wear one.

Mother wanted to buy some meat for when the Clines come over tomorrow. She is making a real Thanksgiving feast, with mashed potatoes, peas, stuffing, and a turkey! And either Lemon Layer Cake or raspberries with cream for dessert...haven't decided yet.

She complained quietly to herself when she saw turkey was selling for eleven cents a pound. But since we are richer folks and she wanted to make a good impression, Mother bought the turkey with a smile.

Only when she turned around did she notice that horrid piece of clothing—if you should even *call* it clothing. Mother calls it the Gibson look, and "It is very new." The Gibson look is really a corset! But this one looks so tiny *no one* could *ever* fit in it, much less my Mother. I'm not saying she is large, but she isn't *that* small. I think no one is. The corset resembles a skirt in the way that it goes slightly past your hips like that a normal corset would not do. I saw pictures in magazines of what they called the *Gibson Girl.* She looks very pretty, but her waist is *so* small, showing the effects of what would happen if you wear the "latest and most wonderful Gibson look." Of course, the magazine makes it sound as though it is *good* that your waist will be super small and shaped like an hourglass, but I have also read what the doctors say could happen if someone keeps wearing a corset: damaged liver and lungs, tuberculosis, and more.

Worse, Mother had me help her tie it together once we arrived home. Her waist did look smaller, but I could not tie the strings. I pulled and pulled, and even accidentally snapped one with no avail. Mother sighed. "Well, maybe it will fit you. You are growing into a lady, Emelise, and it is time you started dressing like one." I *have* been dressing like one! I wear my hair up and even have slightly heeled shoes! Not to mention my completely lady-like dresses. Am I going to have to wear a wretched *corset* just to become a lady? Then I shall never been one!

So instead of trying to *fit* in the Gibson look, Mother had me help do her *hair* in the new Gibson look. It seems as though everything is *Gibson this* and *Gibson that*. I must admit, though, Mother did look quite pretty with her hair sitting directly on her head and small ringlets framing her forehead all the way to her ears.

In bed...

She has not mentioned the corset to me anymore this night.

Papa and Edward are still angry at each other. Though they don't shout at the table like the other day, they still grumbled and growl when one or the other walks by. I wonder what Edward is going to do. I wonder what *Papa* is going to do. True, he did earn his degree as a teacher of English, and has always wanted Edward to follow his example, but I can tell my brother has no intention of becoming an English teacher, or any teacher in this matter.

I hear Nathan practicing the harp. I think he is beginning to understand how to play it. Maybe I will go down in the parlor and listen.

Sunday, September 2, 1900

The Clines will be here any moment! I will write about how the day went.

Everyone woke up at the crack of dawn and readied for Sunday mass. Everyone, that is, except Edward. He stayed in his room and sulked, completely ignoring Papa's orders to get ready. Mother cried, begging, "Edward, please!"

He did not come. I mean, I get how he is angry at *Papa*, but does he have to be mad at God? I prayed during Communion that his soul will not be eternally damned, that he is just going through a tough time and needs to be alone. Even worse, the priest singled out his homily only on Hell and the fires that will consume those who do not follow the Lord's Word. I shrunk in my seat, feeling as if everyone was staring down at me, as if I was the sinner. I don't know about this priest. I like the one in Little Rock better. He didn't shout "Repent! I say, Repent!" so much.

When we arrived home Edward was not there. Yes, Edward is a pain and I sometimes hate him (though I should probably go to Confession for saying that) but he is my *brother*. I can't just forget him and say, "He can take care of himself." I worry.

Mother only sighed. The boys went out to the rabbits (of course), Papa perambulated (isn't that a fun word? Spotted it on a sign) around town, and Nathan practiced his Braille while Mother and I began cooking the grand Thanksgiving feast all for the Clines. This is a list of the food we made:

Roast turkey with lettuce and cherry tomatoes surrounding it
A small plate of steaming roast beef
Buttered beets
Mashed potatoes with white gravy
Vienna rolls

Creamed turnips and peas
Cranberry sauce
Boiled broccoli
Stuffing
Oyster soup
Lemon Layer Cake
Chocolate pudding

 And then for drinks we will have buttermilk, tea, and lemonade. Mother will not allow coffee to be served, even though Papa told her Mr. Cline may crave coffee. She said, and I quote, "Coffee turns your teeth a rotting color. Here we serve tea." I guess Mother wants to make a good impression again.
 So far I think Galveston is everything it ought to be, and the people, too. Nobody has called me snobbish or bossy here (except maybe my brothers, but they don't count). In Little Rock I heard the occasional soul whisper behind my back about "that stuck-up Carson girl" who "thinks because she's rich she doesn't have to listen to other folks." I don't know about that. I mean, I *may* have thought I was better than some people but I was! I didn't live in small house like most of the people. I was lucky enough to be rich. And I guess I wanted to show off? But I have been trying not to do that here. I haven't really had the chance since I have no friends (I don't count Allie May as my friend). But I think moving to Galveston has been the right choice. I was so worried people would call me snobbish here, but I haven't heard a single person gossip at "that stuck-up Carson girl." Maybe they have without my noticing, but so far my worries are fading bit by bit.

 Anyway, the dinner table looked fabulous. My arms ache from glossing it with wood polisher. It now shines like a jewel, though.
 Each placemat is red, and each person gets two glasses, three forks, a spoon, a knife, a napkin, a plate, a saucer, and

there is even a little name card that instructs them where they should sit. Samuel *insisted* sitting by Esther, and Anthony *insisted* sitting by Rosemary. That left me forced to sit by Allie May. Joy.

After everything was set up and the Clines were due in an hour, Edward walked through the door. As he drifted by me—without a word—I smelled something funny. Fish. Clams. Ocean. Why did Edward smell so? Papa wondered the same, I could tell, but did not mention a word, only wrinkled his face in disgust.

I wonder...

Bedtime...

I am going to make this entry short, since it is far past bedtime and I don't want my parents to come up to my room.

Our guests were late in arriving. Mother began to worry the food would grow cold, but just when she was about to send Papa to go looking for them, a knock came at the door.

Mr. Cline started the conversation with numerous apologies, saying he got called in to his work at the last moment for an emergency and it took him a while to get off, and they live all the way over on Avenue Q...

"No need to apologize," Mother assured. Ha! She had *just* been complaining.

Everyone sat at the dinner table and marveled over the food. I, of course, had to sit by Allie May. She hardly even ate anything with all the jabbering she did! About the baby, about fashions, about Galveston. I tried to pay attention, but it was *so* boring I listened to the adult conversation instead.

I couldn't stop staring at Mr. Cline. He spoke about his job as a meteorologist and how he can tell when a hurricane is coming. "That is why I got called into work," he explained. "My crew members insisted a bad storm was arising in the distance, but I assured them it was far too off to tell what kind of storm, and even then it's probably not something to worry about." How assured I felt!

Edward only ate his food, and when he had finished—rather quickly—he scooted his chair back, said, "It was nice to meet you," and marched to his room. How rude! Mother's cheeks flushed with embarrassment and she apologized immensely.

"No need," the Mrs. Cline comforted. Then she began asking Mother questions about how she liked Galveston to far.

Once everyone was done eating, the boys took the younger Cline girls outside to see the rabbits while I showed Allie May my room.

"What's that?" she asked, pointing to my diary I had laying on the desk.

"My diary. I record the days in it."

"Why?" she asked, as if that was the dumbest thing in the world to do.

"Why what? So when I am eighty I can look back and remember what happened today."

"I would rather sew." *Of course you would,* I thought.

Nothing more happened that is worth writing down. I played checkers with Esther (letting her win of course). How she beamed when she jumped me for the last time! Oh, I wish I had a little sister like her.

When it was evening, the Clines insisted they needed to leave. "Next Sunday come to our house," Mr. Cline said handing Papa the address.

What a good day. And to think! Tomorrow Nathan and I get to go to Alice's orphanage! And next Sunday the Clines' for supper! I am glad we moved to Galveston.

I see this entry hasn't really been short.

Monday, September 3, 1900

Papa is going to be calling me soon. I have butterflies in my stomach!

Mother came to me this morning, holding that dreaded corset. "Why don't you put this on, Emelise? You need to look and act more like a lady."

I wanted to shout out, "No! If you want me to act more like a lady, then why do you let me crawl under the porch chasing those stupid rabbits?" But instead I shook my head and said, "Mother, I'm going to an *orphanage* with *Sisters* there. Do you really think they would care if I wore a corset?"

She sighed and said the magic words, "I guess not."

Papa is calling me!! See you soon, dear diary.

Later!!!!

Oh, where to begin? There is so much to tell! Today was the best day in my *life*. I will skip writing about the ride there, since there is so much to tell I don't want to take up all the diary pages describing the trip there. Oh, would you just start writing, Emelise?

St. Mary's Orphan Asylum is three miles away from Galveston, but only a few feet from the Sandy Beach. The orphanage is huge. Papa made sure the driver stopped the wagon far away from the building, respecting the Sisters wishes. Papa then called goodbye, saying he would come back in a few hours.

I couldn't help but stare. Nathan asked me to describe the place, so I will write what I told him. It's like the children live in two mansions: a boys' and a girls'. The girls' is much stronger—I could tell by the way it is built. Both of them are two stories and have many balconies. A small fence stretches around the two dorms, protecting from intruders. The orphanage is nothing fancy. It doesn't have marble lions guarding the door or lampposts uprooting from the ground, lighting up a walkway that isn't even there, or fancy shutters that would enclose the windows.

But, oh, the beach next to it! I could hear the seagulls calling and smell the salty water. I could practically taste the salt! I saw crabs scurrying across the sand, hurrying away to hide from their prey. How I wanted to run in the water, for it was beginning to grow hot out. Wouldn't that be just *divine,* dear diary?

Nathan hooked his arm in mine and we walked towards the palace. In my opinion, the place did look a little haunted. Not a soul in sight…that is, until Alice opened the orphanage door and started running towards us! I hope the Sisters did not spot her doing such an ungodly thing. It is probably a mortal sin for a Sister-to-be to run across the beach towards her family members.

"Emelise! Nathan!" she cried. "You're here! Oh, do come meet the children."

Alice ushered us into the house and introduced us to Sister Elizabeth Ryan. She was a very pretty young woman, Sister Elizabeth, I mean. She had the most caring eyes and a set jaw, along with super smooth skin.

Then I met Sr. Vincent. Two girls were clinging to her dress. One had brown hair with white ribbons, and the other had blond hair with no accessories in it.

After that children came pounding down the stairs, their feet hammering the floorboards and rattling the house.

"Children, please," Sr. Vincent instructed, and they immediately quieted down as they walked towards me and

Nathan. All of them were girls because my brother and I had entered into the girls' dorm. The girls were all sizes! Tall and skinny, short and round. Some had red hair, some had brown, some had blond, and some had black. They wore plain white dresses and plain black shoes, nothing fancy.

It was like a sea of heads consuming me! They asked me questions and tugged on my dress a little, admiring the fancy sewing (I wore my light blue silk dress with white ribbon). "Where did you get that?" "Where do you live?" "How old are you?" On and on!

The older girls—the oldest probably twelve—kept staring googly-eyed at Nathan. He only smiled, obviously not seeing her staring at him with awe. The little ones clung to his leg, and he reached down to pat them.

Sr. Vincent glared at the twelve year old, then said, "Nathan, dearest, why don't you follow me to the boys' dorm? I am sure they would love to meet you."

"I would like to go, too," I insisted. It wasn't that I didn't like playing with the little girls; it was just that I wanted to meet William Murney. He is my age, Alice told me, and wouldn't it be grand if we could become pals?

The three woman—Elizabeth, Vincent, Alice—glanced at each other wearily. Sr. E bent down to my level. "Dear, I don't know if Alice informed you about the rules we have here in this orphanage. As it is true we do let the boys and girls play together occasionally, we hardly ever let a new female guest come in contact with a boy. Do you understand?"

How I didn't want to understand! How I wanted to use my stubbornness and demand to see William! But I didn't. She was a holy Catholic Sister! I couldn't argue. I was lucky enough to even be allowed to come here. I did not want to jeopardize this opportunity.

So instead I nodded, crouched down, and started chatting with a little red head. Sr. Vincent helped Nathan outside and to the boys' dorm (how I wanted to follow him!). Alice, my dear sister, bit her lip and summoned to Sr.

Elizabeth. They walked away for a few moments, talking seriously all the while. I strained my ear to hear, but with the fifty some talkative girls surrounding me, asking me questions, I wouldn't have been able to hear God Himself calling my name if he had shouted it!

    I am tired. Will finish this entry tomorrow.

Next Day...

To continue:

    Alice and Sr. E slowly walked back towards me, making their way through the Sea of Squealing Girls. Alice smiled, as did Sr. E.
    "Children!" Sr. E called, and they, once again quieted down. *Now* I would have been able to hear God if he had *whispered* my name.
    "Children," Sr. E said, "why don't you go follow me outside. We can play in the water. Emelise will soon join us."
    It was only me and Alice standing there once the herd had left. She clapped her hands and hugged me tightly. "Oh, Em! She said yes! You may see William!"
    "What made her change her mind?" Quite quickly I might add.
    "I recalled how depressed William has been these past few days since the death of his parents. I suggested that maybe a visiting age would cheer him up! You may see him. Come, Emelise." How excited I was! Thank goodness Sr. E was not one of those super strict Sisters that didn't listen to a word anyone said.
    I followed Alice outside. The boys' dorm wasn't much different construction-wise except it was, well, bigger and older looking.

We walked inside and right away boys rushed towards me, blurting out questions, same as the girls did. I answered some of them. "I'm thirteen," "Yes, I have a big family," "No, I don't like cabbage" (a little boy asked me that. He quickly told a story about how the Sisters had cooked cabbage and made him eat it and he didn't like it).

"Boys," Alice called out. Just as the girls had, they grew quiet enough to hear a mouse scurrying behind the wall (hopefully there are not any mice in the house…I'm just saying it was super quiet). It was as if the Sisters had so much authority. Wait—I didn't mean it that way, dear diary. *Of course* they do have authority. I am just saying it almost seemed as if no one dared to make a move, for fear of what would happen. Edward would have shouted out, "No. I don't have to listen to you," or something like that. None of these children were brave enough.

Alice continued, "I am taking Emelise to see William. I hear Sister Elizabeth is letting the girls play out on the beach. Don't just stand there! Go out and join them!" And they hurried off, calling out, "Play with us, Emelise!"

"I will in a little bit!"

"Here we are. William's room." Alice opened the door, revealing a quite plain room with simply a bed and bureau. On the bed sat two boys, one of them much older. The older one wiped away tears from the younger ones face and whispered something to him.

I felt like I was intruding. I glanced over at Alice. She did not show any intention of leaving those two boys alone.

"William?" The older boy jumped at the sound of his caretaker's voice. He whispered once more to the little boy, and with a nod the youngster scurried out of the room, not glancing up at us.

"William," my sister said again, "I want you to meet a visitor of ours, Emelise Carson. Emelise, this is William Murney."

The boy cocked his head at Alice, obviously wondering why the visitor was standing in his room, especially a *girl* visitor.

Alice answered, "Sister Elizabeth has given Emelise permission to come see you. You may chat for a few minutes, and then you both will come outside. The children are playing in the water and wish for you to join them. Go along, Emelise."

For some reason, my sister seemed different in these moments. She carried her new role of power well, that I saw. I felt like listening to her right then and there and not questioning her say. Maybe that is how the orphans feel.

Alice left me and William alone. I felt sort of awkward at first. I mean, she had just left me alone with a *boy.* Now, if Kate were here she would probably be gushing over him and fluttering her eyelashes and talking in his high-pitch voice. I don't do that with boys. If I happen to have a boy as a friend, we are *just* friends, thank you. But I do admit he was handsome. He had brown hair and kind eyes.

I stood there, wondering what I would ask him. The thought of his parents flashed through my mind, and I so wondered… But there was something about the way he looked at me told me he had seen depressing images and did not wish to repeat them.

"So…" I started uncertainly, "How old are you?" I knew the answer, for Alice had told me not five minutes ago, but it was all I could think of to start a conversation with a *boy.*

"Thirteen." His voice cracked. Maybe this wasn't a good time. I mean, he had just been almost crying with whom I assumed was his little brother.

"You?" he asked.

"Thirteen."

"Have any brothers or sisters?" he asked.

"Yeah, four brothers and one sister. Alice is my one sister."

"You mean the Alice who volunteers here?" his eyes flashed eagerness now, and I thought we were getting somewhere.

"Yep." Ha. I puffed up like a proud rooster.

"She is so nice!" he stood up now and walked towards me, grinning away. "And she has a beautiful voice. I can hear her singing to the little ones at night."

How proud I grew! Then I made the mistake of saying, "Yeah, they probably miss their parents."

William frowned and turned away from me.

I stuttered, "I'm sorry." My face probably flamed red with embarrassment.

"It's all right," he said, but I knew it wasn't. He started talking then, as if a door had opened. I prayed it would not slam shut. "It was bad enough seeing Mama suffering with the tuberculosis. She didn't eat; didn't talk; just lay there, as pale as the pillow beneath her head. She slept mostly, but when she did wake she continuously said she loved us, and to be good, because Jesus was calling her Home early. But when Papa died… I looked up to him, you know. Respected him."

"I'm sorry," I said again, feeling rather uncomfortable.

"You grow up fast when your parents die and you have to take care of your younger brother. My older sister doesn't live in Galveston. I wish I could see her. You're lucky, Emelise."

Lucky? He thought *I* was lucky? I mean, I guess I get it. I have parents and siblings, but apparently William did not know Edward very well. Sometimes, I would give anything to see Edward leave for a *long* trip—and maybe get lost on he way and have to spend the night in the woods. Then maybe he would get bitten by *loads* of mosquitoes. *Then* he could come back home.

William and I didn't say much then. He apologized for being so straightforward, and said he hoped to be friends. I said I would like that very much.

"Come on," he said, once again happy. "The Sisters will be calling for us soon."

It was so much fun playing on the beach with the ninety-three children! The ten Sisters laughed and laughed, and I began to wonder which ones had objected to the orphans playing in the water, as Alice had said, for all seemed to be enjoying the good time we had.

My, oh, my, the children just *adored* Nathan. I even saw him giving the little red haired girl a piggy-back ride! She laughed and called, "Giddy-up, horsy!" Then Nathan would collapse in the sand, ten children—boys and girls—tackling him. It's those sorts of times that I have trouble believing Nathan is blind.

I chatted with some of the older girls. One of the twelve year olds, Sarah, I recall, whispered about Nathan to me. She asked, "He is rather handsome, don't you think?" then would erupt in giggles. I nodded, agreeing I thought he was handsome, but did not say anything more. I seriously doubt the Sisters would agree with Sarah talking about such things.

William and I played in the water. He would splash me, I would get him back. Then his little brother joined us! We were soaking wet by the time Sr. E called us over, saying my father was here to pick me and Nathan up.

I almost cried saying goodbye to those dear, sweet children. A little brown haired girl, Anna May, *did* cry and hugged my leg, begging, "Do come back soon, Emelise! And bring Nathan, too!" I promised I would try, then glanced up to the Sisters to make sure what I had said was true. Sr. E nodded, which I hope is a sign that I may visit again!

All ninety-three children, ten Sisters, and Alice stood on the porch, calling farewell. I waved until I thought my arm would fall off.

Now Tuesday...

The days are extremely hot, I must mention. Fall doesn't seem to be in sight. Yesterday it reached 97 degrees and it was *so* humid. I could have passed out. Papa said I did look a little discolored and told me to sit in the shade with a glass of cold lemonade. I felt slightly better.

    The way Galveston looks on these exasperating days is quite humorous. Pedestrians shuffle through town, barely able to walk. The women weakly hold up their sun umbrellas, the heat having absorbed all the strength they have. The men fan themselves with their hats, sweat trickling down their face. There is a slight stench throughout the town, but it is hard to notice since it seems as thought no one has the energy to sniff. I would *like* to go to the Pagoda Bathhouse, but Mother says that is no place for a lady to go. Ugh.

    Even in the newspaper it says people all around the globe are being affected by this heat wave. Sometime in August three Philadelphian children were killed after they fell from a fire escape, hoping to catch a breeze. And Mother says that Saturday in New York thirty people died from heat prostration.

    Luckily there is the rain to cool everything down, at least until the heat comes once again and it gets humid. As I write this, I hear rain pounding on the roof. Probably just a little pickle shower. But it would feel just lovely to jump in the puddles.

    You know what, dear diary? The thought of the rain cooling my sweaty skin sounds so good I shall put this pen down and go play in the rain. Maybe the boys want to come along with me.

Still Tuesday…

What a fun time Anthony, Samuel, and I had running through the rain puddles. Mother called us in early, though, for fear of lightning. There was none! I also got a good scolding about how ladies don't run through rain puddles. Fine. Then I simply am not a lady. I am a girl. Ha to Mother.

Papa told us at supper he had some more good news. "I have a job!" he exclaimed. "Carson family, you are looking at the new English teacher of the First District School on 11th Street."

"Oh, James!" Mother cooed. "How lovely."

"And there's more," Papa said, glancing at Edward. "Since school quite soon, I once again spoke with the principle of The Galveston University. He said Edward may come to the university nine o'clock sharp this Saturday morning to take the qualifying exam."

Edward gritted his teeth, "And what if I don't *want* to take the qualifying exam?"

Papa shook his head. "It doesn't matter. You're taking it. That university is the best here in Galveston, not to mention the most expensive. This would be very good for your future, son."

With that, Edward stormed out of the room, mumbling under his breath. I looked sideways at my father. He sighed. It is when he is sad that I can see those wretched scars. I don't know what it is, but whenever he is depressed his wounds seem to show more than when he is laughing. I couldn't bear looking at them. I turned my head as flashes of the blood-stained road entered my mind.

Wednesday, September 5, 1900

I am so mad! You know what Mother went out and did this morning? Guess, dear diary. It is horrid! She went and bought herself tickets to that Tremont Opera House! She bought *two* tickets!

Here is what she told me: "Emelise, you are changing into a young lady, and it is far time you started acting more like one. These opera tickets are for this Saturday night. You are coming along with me."

"But, *Mother!*"

"Emelise," she said firmly, "no complaining. I want you to dress up in your very finest for this night." I hate opera! No, I *despise* it! Even worse, Mother said this as she walked out the door, "You will be wearing the Gibson look."

Not the dreaded corset that is so small I will suffocate!

I tried to protest, but Mother would not have it. "End of conversation," she said. Saturday is only three days away! Maybe I will run away from home and live with the Clines. They are nice enough people. Esther would love having me as her big sister.

Oh what am I saying?! I can't run away from home. I got to think of something else, dear diary. *Fast!*

Later…

Nothing! Are you thinking, dear diary? I need ideas!

Later Still...

I received a letter! From William! Mother stared uncertainly at me as I took the letter and ran up to my room to read it in private. I must admit, I did feel rather strange reading a letter from a boy. It helped take my mind off my worries of the opera house, though!

> *Dear Emelise,*
>   *Your sister Alice gave me your address. You may be reading this with some uneasiness, but there is no need for that. I just wished to say that I thank you for coming to see me personally last Monday. You must be stubborn if the Sisters* actually *allowed you in the boys' dorm!*
>   *Everyone is still chattering on about you and Nathan and the fun they had. My brother hasn't spoken that many words since before my parents' death! I really appreciate the little visit, Emelise, more than words can say.*
>   *I hope you can come visit us soon!*
>
>   *Your forever friend,*
>   *William Murney*

Signed *your forever friend*. My very first absolute true friend since the move! I am so happy. I dearly hope I can visit them soon. Maybe I can say Alice needed my help at the orphanage and oh, what a pity, she needs my help the exact time of the opera. Guess I can't go, Mother.

Thursday, September 6, 1900

Oh, dear diary, do I have some juicy news for you!

I decided to walk around town today, see the sights and try to think of a way to get out of going to the opera.

I went to the harbor. It was quite a long walk, but I figured sticking my feet in the ocean would do me well. Besides, a very nice old man offered me a ride in his carriage, for he just happened to be going that way. Saved me half the trip.

The harbor was magnificent. Big steam ships floated in the water, their grace astounding anyone who happened to stroll by. Their elegant, dove-colored sails flapped in the breeze, mirroring onto the ocean. The beautiful names of her majesties scrolled elegantly across the side, all curly-q. The water splashed onto the sides of the ships, a sweet and soothing sound. Seagulls called out, dipping, diving, soaring through the wind.

Only, there was one problem: the air smelled horribly like clams and fish. Ugh. I wanted to plug my nose. What was I doing there, anyway? A young lady like me walking to the harbor where sweaty, shirtless men worked pulling up clam nets from the ocean? Besides, I wasn't exactly completely acquainted with the thrilling, colorful town of Galveston quite yet. Who know what lay around the bend?

Just when I thought to turn around, I felt faint. It must have been 100 degrees today. I quickly walked away from the fishing boats to the end of the pier and sat. I untied my boots, pulled off my stockings, and slowly slipped my legs into the ocean. How heavenly the water felt! Cool and delightful. Right then I didn't care if the air smelled like clams. I intended on staying for a while.

But then I heard voices behind me. At first I paid no attention.

"You're a good worker," a gruff voice said.

"Thank you, sir," answered a familiar voice, which sent my mind to work, figuring out who had said that. Papa? I didn't dare turn around, for fear they would see me and tell me to shoo on home or maybe they would leave, carrying their conversation with them.

"You're sure you got no kin?" Gruff Voice questioned.

"No, sir. Not here at least. I hope to earn enough money to head back to my hometown where I have someone waiting for me."

"Relative?"

"Not exactly, but someone I care deeply about."

Gruff Voice laughed. "We all have that someone. Come; let's talk business."

"Yes, sir."

I couldn't help it. I turned around and gasped so loud I thought they would wonder who had made that sound. Edward! My brother Edward Carson had been the one talking to Gruff Voice! A million questions ran through my head. What was he doing here? Why did he say he had no family in Galveston? Was he planning on earning money to go back to Little Rock?

Could Edward be working at the harbor hunting for clams to earn enough money to go back to Little Rock and see Ruth Henry? This also explains the horrid stench Edward had on his clothes these past few days.

I am positively shocked. Edward has never worked a day in his life! Yes, back in Little Rock he may have done a few odd jobs at Kate's father's Mercantile, but clam hunting? At the harbor? I told you this was exciting news, dear diary!

Oh, what am I to do? If I tell Papa, Edward will kill me. Literally. He'll kill me then run away, not even coming to my funeral. But if I don't tell Papa, then Edward may leave to

Little Rock without a word. I will *have* to admit I knew something about his little scheme. Then *Papa* will kill me.

Evening…

Why is it always Edward's secrets that must linger in my soul and stay there? Why not a secret of Nathan's? Something crazy even. Maybe Nathan wants to be a famous piano player and compose his own music. A *semi-sightless* piano player.

  Not only that, but his secrets are bad. These ones are the ones that make you feel just as guilty as he should feel. And man, am I shaking. What a secret I am keeping! If Papa ever found out I had kept this from him… Or worse! If *Edward* ever found out what I knew!

  I can't write. I shall set this pen down and think. No, what I really should do is pray. Pray that when Edward murders me it won't hurt too badly.

Friday, September 7, 1900

Still agonizing over the information I know. I wish I would have just turned around instead of gone to that harbor. That way, when Edward ran away I could truthfully tell Papa I did not know anything.

  Even worse, Papa was so happy today, for tomorrow morning Edward will take his exam to enter the university. He even went to the store and picked a suit out for his son! It is a very handsome suit, with black vest, jacket, pants, white shirt, and a black bowtie. Oh, how Papa beamed when he held the suit up to his oldest son.

  "Are you nervous?" he asked. "Don't be. You are going to do just fine."

"I'm not nervous because I'm not taking the exam," Edward declared, crushing Papa's happiness.

"You *are* taking the exam. End of conversation."

Later...

I almost fainted today.

Maybe it is boring to you, dear diary, to mention the weather. But I think I must tell you how exasperated I am with this heat. Again around 100 degrees. Anthony and Samuel spent the entire day fanning the three rabbits. The men were sweaty and smelled. I even sprayed Nathan with some of my perfume! With him knowing of course. I threatened to shove him in the Gulf of Mexico if he did not smell better, so he allowed me to, laughing the entire time. Mother tried not to show her displeasure in the heat. When I said, "I am sweating like a boy!" she snapped back, "Ladies do not sweat." I simply do not understand how she can express that statement with such sureness. *Everyone* sweats *including* girls, ladies, women, and the like.

I forgot to mention this the other day. School will be starting September 10. I am nervous! Luckily I do not have to take an entrance exam like Edward does. I wouldn't fail, though, since I am rather smart. At least I like to think so. Though one time last semester, I boasted on how well I would do on this test. I spent no time studying, saying it would be so easy. Ha! I guess you can sort of figure out what happened, dear diary. I failed the test. Complete F. Or maybe even an F- if there is such a thing. I don't think I got more than three answers correct. I was so embarrassed I stayed in my room six whole days. Nathan kindly brought me each meal until I earned enough courage to walk outside again.

Later again!

I sure am writing in this diary a lot! If I keep this up, I will have it filled by Christmas. Then what shall I do?

Anyway...

That horrid weight with Edward's secret is lifted off my shoulders!

As I was sitting on the porch, Nathan came out and sat with me. For some reason, he asked if I had something on my mind that I would like to talk about. I don't know how he knew, but he did.

So I told him. Everything. From walking to the harbor when I wasn't exactly supposed to, to the conversation between Gruff Voice and Edward, to my horrid fears that Edward will murder me if he finds out what I know. And—*and*—I mentioned the tiny little fear that even though Edward hates me, if he leaves I will miss him. Slightly.

As sweet as Nathan is, he didn't scold me for heading to the harbor, or snap at me for not relaying the conversation to Papa, or laugh with the thought that Edward will kill me, or even taunt me when I said I will miss my oldest brother.

First, he reassured me that Edward would not kill me, because who would he tease then? If anyone else had said such a sentence, I would have marched away all huffy. But when Nathan said it, I laughed and realized he is right.

Second, he said he himself will give it some thought, then tell Papa. My wonderful brother mentioned that *he* will tell Papa and I won't need to. I love Nathan!

Then he asked, "Want to go practice the piano? Now when you hit the wrong keys it doesn't sound *too* bad."

I rolled my eyes, groaning. "No!" We erupted in laughter.

One more bit before bed…

Saw a black cat. Some people say it is bad luck to see a black cat. Ha! I always laugh. People also have said, "Walking under ladders and breaking mirrors is bad luck as well." Ha again. I have walked under numerous ladders just to prove them wrong and purposely dropped a hand mirror on cement to show I am positive that those stupid superstitious are just that—stupid.

Saturday, September 8, 1900—Very early

I am sitting on my balcony, watching the sun rise. It is super early, but I don't mind because this morning is especially wonderful.

  The sky is made of such vivid bright colors it almost seems unreal. Unbelievable bright red illuminates the sky while dashes of rainbow colors blend in. Dazzling pink (I know that is not a color of the rainbow, but anyway). Soft violet. Eye-catching orange. Calming blue.

  It seems so peaceful. But there is a strange stillness I feel when I sit here. I can't decipher it, though. Almost like the moment before a storm. When the clouds are gathering energy to release it the moment before and all is calm, all is still.

  I just remembered that one Christmas song "Silent Night, Holy Night." How it matches to this moment (despite the fact that in the song it is night, but you get the idea). *Silent Night, Holy Night. All is calm, all is bright.*

Later...

Bad news!

Papa woke up just as early as I did this morning and commented on the sky as we ate breakfast. Only he stopped talking when he noticed Edward was not sitting at his usual place.

"He must have needed to take a walk to calm his nerves before the big test today," Papa suggested.

Later, Papa walked into the parlor where we all sat and held up a piece of paper. "I just found this. It's from Edward," he said. He began to read it aloud. "Papa: I have left. There is no need to follow me. I will be fine. Edward."

I felt as though all the air had been sucked out of my lungs. Edward! Gone! Everyone—except Nathan, that is—looked happy, including Papa.

"What a relief! He has changed his mind about taking the exam after all."

He didn't get it. He didn't understand. Papa thought...he couldn't think that...oh no. I almost felt like crying. I glanced at Nathan and he motioned me to the kitchen.

"Nathan, what are we going to do?" I wailed. He paced, his cane thumping on the floor.

"I was going to tell Papa today," he explained. "But Edward was one step ahead of me."

"It's all my fault!" I cried. I never thought I would cry over Edward, but I did then. "If I would have just told Papa about Edward the day I heard that conversation, than none of this would have happened."

Nathan placed his hands on my trembling shoulders. "Edward is a very stubborn brother. He will be fine on his own. Don't worry, Emelise. It was not your fault. Get that out of our head, you hear? *Not* your fault."

Nathan told me he will tell Papa as soon as they are sure that Edward did run away and didn't head to the university like normal. I dearly hope that my brother had a change of heart and went to the university early, but I don't think so.

Later...

I tried to tell Papa. Even though Nathan told me not to, I tried. But, of course, he was so excited that his son had had a change of mind and was going to take the examination after all. I prayed he was actually right about that.

I don't want to be gloomy all day, so I will try to write about something else. But what is there to say?

After finding something to write about!!!!

I am such an imbecile! How could I have forgotten???? All my aches and worries about Edward seem to have completely vanished after this news. Dear diary, everything seems so exhilarating these days! Can't I have *one* calm, not busy day?

Papa, still so excited, was *skipping* around the house today right before lunch. He came up to Mother and said, "How about you and I go to a restaurant and celebrate our son's achievements?"

Mother sighed. "I would love to, James, but Emelise and I have plans this afternoon." She turned to me. "Remember? We are going to the opera. I have your dress all laid out for you. The Gibson look, too. Maybe I could fix your hair?"

Opera! Gibson look! Not the Suffocating Corset! I forgot all about it! What about my plan? My idea to get out of it?

I turned to Papa with plead in my eyes. Maybe he could help.

He glanced my way, knowing full well how much I hated the opera. "Lillian, maybe you and I could go to that show. Emelise can stay here with the children. We haven't had a time alone for quite a while now. And school will be starting soon and I will be gone all day. Come on."

"But I had everything planned," Mother complained. She seemed just as stubborn as I am at that moment.

"And everything will still be planned, only a different person will be going with you."

"But, James…"

"*Lillian.*"

That did it all. Mother threw up her hands and sighed. "All right! We'll go." I rushed to her and threw my arms around her. I did not need to go to the opera! Strike up the choir and sing the hallelujah chorus!

Mother said, "Don't you dare think you are getting out of this, young lady. You are wearing the Gibson look tomorrow evening when we have supper with the Clines."

Yeah, yeah, yeah. Sure, sure, sure. I didn't listen. Getting out of the opera show with my mother clogged my ears from the world around me.

Papa clapped his hands and ran up to his room. "Go dress in your very best, my darling! We are going to eat at the finest restaurant in Galveston then head to that opera show!"

Now both of my parents are gone. It is almost noon. Before Mother left she tried to back out of it. "Look at the weather, James. Dark clouds? What if there is a thunderstorm? The boys will be frightened."

Papa assured her they would be fine. "Now could we please hurry?"

"Yes, yes, yes. We're leaving. Listen to Nathan, children! Edward should be back soon."

Listen to Nathan? Of course. Edward back soon? I dearly hoped so.

Now we are home alone. Just Nathan, Anthony, Samuel and me. Yay! Yay! No parents to listen to.

Later...

The weather has picked up from just a few hours ago. It is beginning to get quite windy, and the rain is really coming down. The sky is very dark with patches of blue sewed in here and there (don't you love that wording, dear diary? *Sewed in*). It seems so different from this morning, when the sky was all tranquil and colorful. Now it's menacing and dark.

But it is sort of thrilling. I always find thunderstorms exciting. Like a good book.

Oh, Anthony and Samuel are calling me. I shall go see what they want.

Later again...

Writing this outside on the porch while Nathan sits next to me and the boys play in the street. There are no worries of them being hit by a wagon since the streets are deserted from those contraptions and here is why: The storm seems even worse now. I mean, not bad enough that I cannot sit outside, but unusual. The rain comes in bits, stopping and then going again. But what is even more peculiar is that the streets are flooded—literally flooded. I know it is pouring super hard sometimes, but I don't think it is raining hard enough to flood the streets a few inches. I even walked down the street in the direction of the Gulf and saw an amazing sight. Those people's yards were filled with water. Not a few inches like ours, but a few feet. Children splashed around, yipping and hollering. Even ladies waded knee deep through the water.

Now I wonder: All of this could not simply come from the rain could it?

Stop worrying so much, Emelise. It is just a mere thunderstorm. If it were anything bad, we would have received some sort of warning, would we not? Besides, the newspaper reported it would be rainy and windy today, nothing more.

I watch Anthony and Samuel play in the water. They have constructed paper sailing ships and are gently placing them in the water, then watching them sail down the street. Some sink, while others manage to travel quite far.

I paused my writing to take a look at what Samuel spotted. Frogs! Lots and lots of frogs are hopping through the street, trying to stay on the few dry parts. Those hundreds of frogs scurrying by look like a moving carpet.

My brothers seem to be having fun. Maybe I will join them. It seems everyone else has—the whole town practically. Running through the water with no shoes could feel heavenly, especially after this big heat wave.

Sitting inside...

I called the boys inside once it began to get super windy. Honestly, I am scared. Being home alone isn't as pleasurable as I thought it would be. Nathan quietly plays the piano, but I see him occasionally pausing to listen to the thunder. Anthony and Samuel try to play checkers, but they hide under the blanket when the rumbling gets to loud.

Fear also rushes through my bones about the little children at St. Mary's Orphan Asylum. Poor Anna May! She begged me to come visit her soon, and so far I have not kept my promise. Maybe I can visit her on Monday. Or better yet, tomorrow, Sunday. Nathan must come to, of course. The little ones adored him.

And I also want to see William again.

Oh my goodness! The wind! It is shaking the rafters of this house harder than I have ever heard it.

The boys are peering over my shoulder, whispering, "What's going on? What's going on?" My hands are shaking. What *is* going on?

After talking with Nathan...

Nathan and I have decided something.

We are going to try and find Mother and Papa. My brother agrees this storm is going to get no better and he fears for the worst. Worst as in what? I want to ask.

Call us crazy, dear diary, but you aren't here. You don't understand what I am going through right now. I am scared. Terribly scared.

We shall look for them at the Tremont Opera House. Please, Sweet Jesus, let them be there. Please, please, please.

About thirty minutes later…

We didn't make it.

As the four of us left, I grabbed the boys' hands and towed them along with me. A and S cried, begging me to turn around because they were frightened. Nathan looked just as apprehensive as I. But I wouldn't do it. If the storm continued to grow worse, I wanted my parents to be home to experience it with me.

The rain batted us fiercely. A and S wailed. They tried to cover their faces with their hands. I almost wanted to cry as well. It felt like hail. I thought I would be bruised.

We waded through the water. It wasn't ankle deep anymore. It was knee deep. There was also a current. A big one. It pulled us the opposite direction we wanted to go.

Once, Samuel fell. His head went under the water. I screamed his name, but he did not bob back to the surface. Nathan held a screeching Anthony back while I frantically *dived* into the water to try and find him. I thought I had lost my little brother forever.

Only when I almost gave up did I hear him calling my name. "Emmie! Emmie! Please help! Please help!"

"I'm coming Samuel!" I shouted back, trying to wade through the water in his direction. He had drifted a ways down the river, and now was clinging to a picket fence. When I reached him we embraced, tears of joy streaming down our faces.

"I want to go home, Emmie. I'm scared." His little voice pierced my heart like a sword.

"Soon, Samuel. Soon. Just a little bit more."

But the opera house wasn't a little bit more. I felt completely turned around. Nathan was holding onto my shoulder, while I held Samuel's hand, and Samuel held Anthony's. I dragged the trio through the water, trying to find my bearings.

Then I gave up. *Maybe they are already home*, I hoped against hope. We turned around, this time the current pushing us and making us lose our step. Since I was the leader, if I went down we all would go down. I tripped, which dragged the boys and Nathan under the water with me. I will never forget that feeling. A frightened, panicked feeling. My lungs screamed for air. Though the water was only knee deep, it was strong and forced us down.

When I thought I would drown all four of us, someone grabbed my shoulder angrily and pulled us up. A man—a very grumpy looking one—shouted, "What are you kids doing here? Get to safety!"

Anthony cried, "We're lost!" I nodded in agreement.

"Where do you live? Give me your address."

I told him, and the man sighed. "That's far away. You *are* lost. Grab onto my jacket and follow me. I'll take you there."

Finally we reached home. I thanked the man. As he ran back into the flooded street he shouted, "Make sure you get to safety. This storm is going to be a nasty one!"

That frightened me out of my wits.

My parents are not here. Neither is Edward. Now I am sitting in the parlor by the fire Nathan has started. We have changed clothes, and our old ones are drying. Anthony and Samuel's lips are still blue. That water was so cold.

Thunder again. How long is this storm going to last? More important, how bad is this storm going to get?

Still Saturday...

A family has joined us—a husband, wife, and son. He looks to be about seven. The son, I mean. They came knocking at our door. Pounding really. At first I thought it was my parents until an unfamiliar voice kept shouting, "Open up! Open up!" As frightened as I was, I didn't want to open up the door. The rain was still hammering down on the roof tiles and the house still shaking like a leaf. What would happen if I answered the man's pleas? Would he rob us? Order us out of the house?

He let himself in. We were all crowded around the fireplace, trying to get warm when I assumed he thought no one was home and just opened the door and walked right on in, his little family trailing behind him.

The man stopped in his tracks and stared bewildered at us. "Who are you?" he asked, as if this was his home and we were intruding.

I stuttered a reply. "I'm Emelise Carson. I live here."

"Live here? Well then you won't mind if we stay for a spell until this wretched storm lets up?"

I didn't answer because he didn't wait for an answer. He shrugged off his rain coat and helped his wife and son get more comfortable in the parlor. They didn't even introduce themselves, as if once the storm is over they would march out of this house and forget all about us and why did we need to know names?

The man is wearing a suit, I see now as I write this by firelight, and looks to be some sort of salesman, considering the fact that he is hugging a large briefcase to his chest.

The Mrs. is wearing a purple gown with white lace, and possibly the Gibson look because it looks like her waist is unusually small.

The son is also wearing a brown suit, though it is rather soaked and spoiled now.

But something just doesn't seem right about this family. For instance, Mr. won't let go of his briefcase for a moment. When Anthony asked what was in it, he didn't answer and just stared at the fire. Mrs. is quite jumpy and—how should I put this?—hysterical. She continues to pet her son whispering, "The storm will be over. The storm will be over." Her eyes are scary. They dart around.

Oh, who am I to call people names? I am terrified out of my mind as I write this. The ink is spilling all over the page. I don't know how much more I can take. Surely Mother and Papa would have wanted to be reunited with us, correct? Why are they not here then?

Later—around four in the afternoon

Something strange is going on. I walked out onto the porch, wanting to get away from that unusual family. The water was rising. Rising as I watched it. It was increasing so fast.

Then I went out into my yard, my legs surrounded by water. The rain continued to pound down on my back, almost as if someone threw rocks at me. How it stung!

I then did a peculiar thing. I stuck my fingers in the water and brought it up to my mouth, tasting it. It couldn't be. This was not rain water. This was salt water. Pure salt water. But how? I watched closely the movement of the water for the first time. No. It couldn't be. It almost seemed as if the Galveston Bay and Gulf of Mexico were combining, forming together. That could only mean one thing. This was not a normal storm. But why didn't anyone in town send out a signal, some type of warning to the residents? It couldn't be *that* bad could it? But why then would the whole town be covered in knee deep salt water?

Later...

Something is definitely wrong. We are all huddled in the parlor, so, so frightened. Our flooring is full of holes, and here is why: The Mr. noticed the water outside and shouted out, "We need an axe. Find one. We need to chop holes in the flooring." I was taken aback.

"Why?" Not the beautiful mahogany flooring!

"I read it in a book. Now where's an axe?!" Of course, let's starting ruining the flooring of my home just because you read it in some fairytale! I tried to stop him, but he frantically started running through *my* house and throwing around *my* pots and ruining *my* furniture until he found the axe in Papa's room under his bed. Most hysterically, he darted into the parlor, with a white-knuckle grip on the axe's handle. His tall shadow danced around on the walls, like some dark monster breathing heavily that would soon do something murderous. I saw the look in his eyes. He was crazy. Insane. I don't blame him, though. Who wouldn't be in a time like this?

The man heaved the axe up and over his head, only a few feet away from my brothers and me. Horrid thoughts flooded my mind. I feared the worst was about to happen.

"Anthony! Samuel! Get back!" Without warning, the man swung the axe onto the parlor floor. It stuck into the boards. He did it again. Heaved, swung, stuck. Chips began flying, and I commanded A and S to cover their eyes. Soon holes large enough for a rat to crawl through littered our flooring. A and S began to cry uncontrollably, and Nathan hurried over to my side, placing his hand on my shoulder. Water erupted through holes like a fountain. Within ten minutes an inch of water was covering the floor. Mr. sat down on the sofa, panting heavily.

I am so, so worried. Why were there holes in the floor? Why did the rain continue to fall but the flood water taste like salt? Why hadn't anyone warned us about this oncoming storm and the newspaper had just said, *Rain with extreme wind*?

Later…

Lord, save us! The wind isn't stopping! The water is rising!

It is morning. Devastation surrounds me. I sit here, on the street curb, covered in blood and injuries.
  But what has happened? What is the date? I can't write. I can't remember.

Is it still the same day? Or did I just write that a minute ago? I recall…the water intensifying, the wind increasing. *Why can't I remember anything?*

Nathan, Anthony, and Samuel are here with me. We are sitting by our house. I think our house. There is nothing left. People wander by, half dazed by what has happened. What *has* happened? No one is talking. Everyone walks around half dead, half asleep. There is this eerie silence enveloped throughout the town. I feel nothing. I am numb. Cannot write.

We only wander around town, knowing not where we go. How many days have gone by? I cannot think. Anthony and Samuel do not cry, do not speak. Their faces are bruised, their skin cut and bloody. Nathan…something is wrong with him. It is as if a wall is surrounding him. He does not notice anything I tell him, anything I do. I worry.

My strength is increasing. I can write more, though I do not know the date. I want to tell you, dear diary, what has happened. But I cannot. My memory is not working. I can only describe what I see.

Disaster. The only word for it. Buildings are piles of lumber, nothing more. Wood litters the street. But the businesses, houses… I cannot write. I am numb.

I shall try again. There is nothing left of them. It looks as if someone just dumped large piles of wood all over the place. The roofs melt like candlewax over the broken homes. Crucifixes from churches hang out of the backs of the wall. Signs are no longer hanging. Carriages are tipped over. Telephone poles are sprinkled over the town as if a giant monster had dropped his toys. Remaining residential areas stick out like a cardinal among crows. Almost as if those few untouched areas had the Hand of God protecting them, shielding them. Why did the All Loving, All Merciful God protect the Cotton Mill but not our home? Why did He allow *presentable* buildings to be as hard to find as a flower in the winter? Why did He allow the town to look like a giant stepped on it and decapitated bodies to be as common as lace on a dress???

There is nothing. The best a person can hope for is if the roof of their house is still in-tack. They cannot hope for their fish-scale tiles to still be nailed to the walls, or their porch to be hooked onto the door, or the windows to be clear and clean. Nobody can hope for anything. Not anymore. Not after what happened.

I am slowly getting my memory back. That must mean it has been many days since that one. That Day that started out perfect and beautiful and colorful and finished a disaster. That One Day…

I remember seeing a black cat. Two days before That Day? One day? Black cats mean bad luck, I think. So is this my fault? Since I saw the evil animal?

I am hungry. Maybe that is a good sign. My brothers will occasionally allow me to help them drink some fresh water, but they do not respond.

    I fear none of us can eat, though. Not with the terrifying sight before our eyes every minute of every day. Anthony and Samuel do not cry. Maybe I have mentioned that. They sit there, their lips forming words but nothing coming out. I want them to speak and I want Nathan to stop being unresponsive. I want That Day to never have happened.

I still remember nothing about That Day. Or anything else. We moved to Galveston, did we not? And Papa was going to get a job as an Algebra teacher? No, English teacher. But what of them? What of my parents? What of my other brother…Edward? And my sister? Alice? What of them? Where are they? Where is my memory?

What is the date?

I saw a frightening man today. He had no arms and half a face. And he was still alive. I was walking around the used-to-be town of Galveston, Texas—just a little, not too far away from my un-talkative brothers—when I came around a corner and ran right into him. I screamed so loud. He had no shirt on, for one, and that clearly showed his missing arms, all the way up to his elbows. They bled lightly. The right side of his face was bruised, cut, bloody, and partly missing. He had no ear. No skin for the right forehead. No right part of his lip. I was shocked he was still living.

He grinned, then laughed. I think he had gone crazy. His head tilted back and he let out a big chuckle. "Did I scare you, little lady?" he asked, his speech slurred for lack of a mouth to use. He laughed again.

Then something strange happened. He began to cry. He crouched onto the ground and wailed hysterically. "My wife," I think he said. "My son. My baby Rose. Only three months. She loved to laugh." I just slowly walked away, back to my own little family.

I fear I must take care of A, S, and N on my own. I watch them almost every minute of every day. I worry so very much. I heard there are medical stations planted around, but I do not think they could walk. It seems they are in shock, all three of them—Nathan the most. I want my loving brother back.

There is gossip. I heard a woman say, "It's all that Isaac Cline's fault. He told us not to put up a seawall. We should have never listened to that wretched man. He killed my husband! I'm a widow!"

A man said, "No, I heard he ran through the town, warning the people to take cover."

Another man: "Are you kidding? If he had warned the people like he said he did, then why are my son and daughter dead, swallowed up by the sea?"

Another woman: "I heard it's not even Isaac's fault. I heard it's his brother's fault. Joseph. He's a meteorologist, too, you know. How come he never told us about this storm?"

I do not know what to believe. I remember the Clines. And I worry for them. What of Mr. and Mrs. Cline? How is she fairing, pregnant and all? What of little Esther and

Rosemary, and even Allie May, whom I was never too terribly fond?

What of my sister as well? What of the orphans at the orphanage? Sister Elizabeth? Sarah? Anna May? William? What of my parents?

Something amazing happened today, dear diary. Anthony and Samuel awoke from their sleepy shock.

I was sitting on the curb next to them, praying—though I did not know why since it seems God does not answer my prayers—when I heard Samuel whisper. I jerked my head, and, sure enough, his lips were moving. But this time, instead of silence coming out of those lips, words did. Wonderful words, though I could not understand what he said.

"Samuel?" I asked. "Please speak up."

Gibberish still. "Samuel. *Speak up.* I cannot understand you when you mumble." I so wanted him to say something. And he did.

"Look, Emmie," were his first words. "Freddy. He's escaped. Go catch him, Emmie." I thought he had gone insane, seeing things maybe.

But he said again, "Look, Emmie. Over there." I turned my head and what did I see? A rabbit. A white rabbit with brown ears and brown paws. One of ours. Freddy, Samuel claimed it was. I didn't even worry about it running away. I only stood up, walked over there, and scooped it into my arms. I think it was too shocked to start kicking.

"Here you are, Samuel." I handed him the rabbit.

He smiled and petted it, cooing, "Good boy. I missed you. Where were you? It's supper time."

Samuel's talking must have triggered Anthony's wake up button. He started to blink, then turned his head. He saw the rabbit in Samuel's arm and immediately said, using Samuel's nickname, "Curt! I told you not to take them out of the cage. They could run away and Emmie will get mad again."

Tears of joy filling my eyes, I hugged the boys until they insisted, "You're crushing our bones!" I think they will be all right. I now only worry about Nathan. He does not do anything but sit and stare.

Samuel just asked me, "Emmie, when can we eat? I'm hungry." I will now find the some food, for I am hungry as well.

I almost wish Anthony and Samuel had not awakened from their shock. They cry. I do not blame them. Dead bodies litter the floor and are as common as stars in the night sky. Some hang from trees. Others float in giant water puddles. But it is the way they *look* that is most disturbing. It almost seems as if the water melted away their face and clothes. It is so hard to tell if that is a person you know or not. Some of the corpses are missing arms, feet, and even heads. Glass punctures the skin. Wood sticks out of a body part as if it is one giant splinter.

There is also the smell. Oh, the smell. The scent of rotting flesh is most disturbing.

There are groups called *Dead Gangs* that go around and collect the bodies. They have started to bury them at sea this very day. I heard rumors that the Dead Gangs held fifty black men at gunpoint, forcing them to help drop the bodies into the sea and promising them whiskey if the job was completed.

I wish they would just get the job done so the bodies are not so numerous.

I also wish I would receive word from my parents, Alice, and Edward. Where are they? I have checked the notices and attention signs around town, but there are none for the Carson children. Tomorrow I shall write one of my own for my family.

Maybe I should check the newspaper…

NO. Do NOT think like that Emelise. They are alive. They are well. They will come back.

Same day, I think, as I wrote that last entry. I wish I knew the date. I also wish I could remember what happened That Day. But I cannot.

I decided Samuel and Anthony needed to be checked by a nurse, just to be on the safe side. But I couldn't leave Nathan alone, not in his condition. I then saw a little girl, about eight years old, sitting not too far off from us. I called her over and asked her if she minded keeping Nathan company for a while. She perked right up and began chatting away about her pet cat Susie that had run off and hopefully would return. I think she was half-sane.

Taking Anthony and Samuel down the block to a makeshift hospital, I held them near me, trying to cover their eyes but letting them see well enough so they knew where to walk. It was hard to walk. Very hard. We climbed over houses and stores, churches and cotton mills. Several times we would step and fall into a hole, our legs once again cut. Samuel hugged his rabbit close to him. He refused to leave it with Nathan because "something isn't right with him." How I know.

On the way there, A and S began asking me questions. "When are Mother and Papa coming back?" "When can we see Alice?" "Did Edward run away?" "Is Esther all right?" "What about Rosemary?" "Where are Fuzzy and Fluffy?" I continued to tell them that I did not know. I wish I did.

The nurse at the makeshift hospital—only a couple tents pitched here and there—declared A and S perfectly fine, despite the fact that A had blood running down the side of his head and S had a bruise the size of Texas on his shoulder. When she examined me, she said I probably have a concussion, which is why I cannot remember what happened. She said maybe if I saw a familiar object that was here before the storm came that would jog my memory. But what is there to be familiar with? All we have is gone.

When I returned to Nathan, the eight year old girl was gone, and Nathan was sitting alone, his eyes staring off into another world.

The bodies came back onto the shore this morning. Rumors are flying. It seems as if the workers who threw the bodies in worked too quickly, not taking special care into making sure the people would sink. Now all seven hundred or so decaying bodies look even worse than before, their stomachs and faces bloated, though I do not know why.

I fear the worse is going to happen to them. I hear the Dead Gangs are going to start numerous fires over Galveston and begin burning the bodies. Please, God, don't let that happen—A and S already cry far too much with the sight before their eyes. Listen to me this time and answer my prayer.

It has started. The Dead Gangs march through town, horses pulling wooden carts filled with bodies. Decaying, pale, bloating bodies. It seems as if they don't even care if that person could be identified. They only pick the person up and throw him in the pile, then the horse or donkey pulls the cart to one of the many giant fires growing throughout Galveston.

At first it seemed the idea of burning men, women, and children was very wrong and considered sacrilege. But the Dead Gangs do not care.

I tried to stay away from the giant flames, but had to take a look. I fear I will pay for it with nightmares tonight. I fear I cannot tell even you, dear diary, the sight I saw.

The whole town is enveloped in the stench of burning flesh. It is almost unbearable in the 100 degree weather and the Dead Gangs are throwing decomposed bodies into giant fires.

Nathan is coming around. He eats the little food I have to offer him and drinks ordinarily. But he does not speak. Nor move. Only sits.

I posted a notice for my parents. I was supposed to do it yesterday, but I could not for fear of running into another fire and seeing the sight I saw again.
     Here is a copy of my note:

TO JAMES AND LIILLAIN CARSON: I have Nathan, Anthony, and Samuel here with me. Please, if you read this come to where our house used to be. We are waiting to be reunited with you again. Love, Emelise.

I saw other posts as well. This one broke my heart:

Mommy and Daddy: I have Baby Anna with me. The two of us are fine, though little Johnny does not wake up. Please come back to our home. We miss you. Love, Katy.

And here is a copy of another note:

RYALS—If Myrtle, Wesley, Harry, or Mabel are living, please address their mother, Mrs. Ryals, 2024 N.

Please let me find Mother and Papa. I miss them.

Saw a reflection of myself in a broken mirror. I must be the scariest person alive. My hair is matted, my dress torn and discolored. My arms are scarred and bloody. My face is covered in cuts and bruises. I am no longer the pretty young lady I used to think I was.

Wednesday, September 13, 1900

I now know what the date is. Saw it in the newspaper. Is it really only Wednesday? I don't even feel like continuing to write the days. I shall now only do so occasionally.

When I picked up a newspaper I wish I had not. The *Confirmed Dead* list is so long. It covers a whole page and more. Here are some names that I will write down directly from the newspaper:

RYALS, Charles L. (3916 Avenue R ½)
RYALS, Harry (son of Charles)
RYALS, Mabel (daughter of Charles)
RYALS, Myrtle (daughter of Charles)
RYALS, Wesley (son of Charles)

I fear that Mrs. Ryals will not receive a response to her notice. Her children and husband are gone.

Some whole families have been lost. I saw that a husband, wife, and their seven children all had perished. All seven.

I guess I should consider myself one of the lucky ones. But is anyone a lucky one? Should anyone feel lucky to see the sight before our eyes and smell the burning bodies? Sometimes I wish I would have died in the storm. I would be spared from the wretched sight and smell of burning bodies. I would be spared from seeing my little brothers cry and having to worry about my other siblings and parents even being alive. I would be spared from all of this disaster.

We saw the family of Isaac Cline. I can remember them…but why not the storm? Why not the most important thing that happened? I read the beginning of my diary, and I now remember everything before the storm. *But why not That Day?*

Mr. Cline was holding Esther's hand. Allie May and Rosemary trailed behind him, close to another man who looked similar to Mr. Cline, almost as if they were brothers. They only walked, their eyes staring forward.

Esther saw me and rushed towards me. "Emelise!" she cried. "We can't find Mommy. Where is she? I want her to come back." I did not know what to say. I glanced up at Mr. Cline. He did not acknowledge me.

I couldn't help feeling anger when I stared at Mr. Cline. How I had felt pride at first. How everyone had felt pride and privileged to be able to meet a fine meteorologist of Galveston and have him over for dinner! But now I felt only rage. Why had he not warned us about That Day? Why had he said a storm big enough to destroy Galveston was a *crazy idea?* Why had he assured me nothing would happen a few days before it did happen? I had to turn away, for fear I would start yelling at him. I think the whole town feels the same way. They growl and make faces behind his back. Some call names.

Nathan is awake from his shock. Unlike Samuel who spotted his rabbit, Nathan only started to blink and move around. I cried and hugged his neck. But he did not respond. I looked into his eyes. I waved my hand over them. He did not blink.

"Nathan?" I asked, my voice scared. "Do you see my hand?" He always could, because he could see objects.

"Emelise?" He reached his arm up and grasped my hand. He felt it. Then he cried. "I can't, Emelise. I can't see anything. Everything is black and dark. I see nothing, Emelise. Nothing."

We hugged each other and sobbed. My greatest fear has come true. My brother is completely blind. He must have hit his head and—

Oh, I am so angry!!! GOD WHY DID YOU LET THIS HAPPEN?! Why are you letting my parents be missing? Why do you let Alice and Edward be missing as well? Why did you let Nathan become completely blind? Why did you let this wretched storm happen in the first place and kill infants and giant families? WHY?

Next Day…

A and S have their noses plugged with clothespins. Tears trail down the soot on their faces. S does not let go of that rabbit. He constantly strokes it, asking "When will Fuzzy and Fluffy come home?" I practically shout at him that I do not know.

Nathan cries often. I have never seen him cry. He is always such a good listener and quiet and humble… My eyes fill with tears every single time I look at him.

I also try to comfort him, saying it was a good thing he learned Braille without peeking at the dots and he can still play the piano, violin, and harp. But he doesn't talk to me. There is a large gash on the side of his head, which I believe is where a beam hit him. He is still the handsome young man all the young ladies adored. But I just wish he would act like that young man he was.

Same Day Later…

Some good news (if I should call it that): I am remembering, dear diary. That nurse was right. I did need a familiar object to jog my memory.

I decided to salvage anything I could from the house, so I begin tossing boards and digging through the debris. I cut myself a few times.

It was hard work, pulling out boards from our red and white house—or as Samuel called it, the Carson Candy Cane House—but I persevered. I soon realized I was standing on the place where my bedroom used to be. Hoping to find something of mine, I begin fiercely pulling up the boards. A and S kept asking what I was doing, but I did not answer.

Then I saw something. Green fabric. I ripped the boards away and threw them behind me. Then I saw what it was. My dress. The one I had worn a few weeks ago the night of that thunderstorm. I pulled it out and hugged it. I spread out the skirt and saw the ink stain. I had meant to scrub it so Mother would not notice…

Then the memories flashed. They came flooding into my brain so quickly it hurt. My head throbbed. I closed my eyes. I remembered the beautiful sunset. And the storm. Oh, the storm. I saw the water rushing into my house and breaking my windows. I tasted the salt. I felt the darkness that enveloped us as if we had been swallowed by a monster of some sort. I could hear the cries and screams of innocent neighborhood children soon becoming victims to such an unknown phenomenon that God allowed to happen. My hands grew cold, as if they were in that icy, icy water once more.

I wanted it to stop. I wanted the pictures to stop flashing. All this time I had hoped remembering would help me, but it didn't. It only hurt me. I had never experienced such horror in my life then when those images flickered through my brain. Never such horror. I wanted it to stop! And I even shouted out. But I was forced to remember.

I need to tell you, dear diary, what happened that Saturday night. But not now. My brain still hurts.

It is later. I am going to attempt to write the story. I will start after I wrote that last entry on That Day, pleading to the Lord to save us.

<u>The Storm of 1900—Emelise's Tale</u>

We were huddled in the parlor, the water slowly rising across the entire floor. The rain beat down on our roof. The wind increased. I hugged Anthony and Samuel close, far away from that strange family. The Mr., on the other hand, hugged his briefcase, never letting go. The Mrs. soothingly whispered to her young son, who whimpered.

Then the roof seemed to be lifting off its foundation. It heaved...and fell back down. And heaved...and fell down. I thought for sure the roof would be lifted up and then collapse on us.

At the moment when I thought the house would collapse, Mrs. bolted up and ran to the window. She shrieked ever so loudly. We ran over to see what she had been frightened by. The water for one. It seemed to be three, four, five feet high. Barrels and chunks of wood floated down the current. Only when I saw they were not barrels did I yelp myself. They were bodies. One, two, three—more than I could count. The bodies of citizens of Galveston bobbed up and down in the salty water. A and S began to cry. I yelled at everyone to stay away from the window. I was surprised it had not shattered yet.

Only when we returned to the parlor did the storm seem to pick up immediately. The house shook with such ferocity.

Our beautiful cherry cabinet collapsed onto the floor, water splashing. Silver candlesticks toppled over. Pots, pans, plates, and cups descended onto the parlor floor and floated in the water, resembling the paper sailing ships my brothers had made earlier that morning.

The windows then broke. All fifteen or more of them at the same time it seemed. I could even hear the ones upstairs. Bits and pieces flew through the air towards us. I screamed at the boys to cover their eyes.

They wailed loudly when little pieces of glass punctured their skin and landed in their hair. The Mr. protected his face with his briefcase, and the Mrs. and her child covered up themselves with a blanket, shrieking all the while.

Then the sound of the wind. Oh, the wind. It blew through the house like a tornado had formed directly on top of us. It extinguished the fire we had started. We could barely see.

Mrs. stood up from her chair abruptly again and ran to the now broken window. Rain misted her face. She exclaimed, "The people! They're leaving their houses!"

I instructed my brothers to stay seated in the now two inch deep water and ran over to Mrs. She was right. It must have been close to fifty people in the water. Some tried walking, some floated on doors, while others rode horses (though the horses had as much trouble making it in the water as everyone else).

I thought those people to be crazy. No, utterly stupid. Never could they make it to wherever they were going when the rain felt like nails and the wind could blow you over.

But the Mrs. disagreed with my thoughts. She called to her husband and son, demanding that they must leave the house before it collapsed and possibly head to the YMCA where it will be safer. Her eyes darted. She was insane, I saw.

She did not listen to my pleas to remain, only gathered up her son and husband and marched out the door, the wind almost blowing her back. I stared out the broken window and saw the trio wade through the water. They had only made it a few feet when a piece of wood came flying and knocked the briefcase out of the man's grasp. The briefcase then hit his son. The boy collapsed into the water. He remained still.

The briefcase had popped open and out flowed money. Lots of it. Thousands of dollars. And it all floated into the water. The man quickly gathered up as much as he could—the Mrs. wailing at her son to answer—and carried the limp boy over his shoulder. I watched them until I could no longer see, for the sky had darkened, blanketing the entire city of Galveston like a black shroud.

I returned to my three brothers, hugging them close.

Suddenly, we couldn't *see whatsoever. The power went out. We were all alone while being enveloped in darkness with the wind increasing and the rain pounding on the roof.*

I cannot write anymore. Maybe later.

Later...

I shall try to finish.

The Storm of 1900—Emelise's Tale (Part Two)

We remained clustered together in the darkness. I could feel the water increasing, for it now reached my stomach as I sat on the floor. I told my brothers to sit on the sofa, out of the water.

I did not even pray during those times. I couldn't. I was so frightened I could not even beg for mercy from that All Merciful God.

With the way the water rose and the wind howled, I had long ago figured out that this was not a normal storm. It was a hurricane. The hurricane Mr. Cline had said never would happen. The hurricane he had called a crazy idea. The hurricane no one wanted to put up a seawall to protect the city from. How terrified I grew, but tried not to let my brothers know.

We could not see anything. I then knew what it was like to be blind. To hear sounds and not know what made them. To have something brush your arm and not know what did it. How could Nathan survive such a horrid feeling?

It must have been midnight. We stayed in the parlor the entire time. The water continued to rise. I instructed my brothers to stand on the table in the dining room. It took forever to find the table because of the blackness. We scurried on top of it. But as we did, the water only rose higher, and higher, it soon reaching past our boots. I grew terribly afraid. My one idea had just been ruined. What now?

I did not have time to think. The roof and house started heaving again, as if taking a giant breath. Wood cracked. I feared for our very lives.

Only when I thought for sure the roof would very much collapse directly on us did I remember Mrs. Sealy's house, our neighbor. Her house was definitely strong than ours, anyone could see that. I knew if we stayed here we would eventually die. But if we went outside…

I chose going to Mrs. Sealy's. If it was in fact true that her house would withstand this storm, I wanted to be in it.

Gathering up my two little brothers and semi-sightless big one, I shouted at them that they needed to stay close to me at all times. "Do you understand? Do not let go off my dress. Hold on tightly."

I stood in front of my front door and counted to ten. I would go then. But I didn't. Fifteen seconds went by. Then thirty. Then a minute. Whenever I decided to go, the house would start to breathe again and my fears would replace my boldness.

Go now, Emelise, I thought. Making sure my brother's were hanging on firmly to my dress, I grabbed the brass doorknob and turned it. The door flung open and the wind pushed us back against the wall, my brothers letting go and all of us toppling into the frigid water that had filled my house.

Gasping for air, I tried to find my family. "Anthony! Samuel! Nathan!"

"Over here, Emmie! Here, here!"

Over the wind their shouts sounded like whispers. I splashed in the water, my arms frantically searching since my eyes could not.

"Here, here!" Anthony's voice began to fade. I could not imagine the thought of losing my brothers. The brothers I had sometimes wished I did not have.

I am sorry, dear diary. I fear my tears are blotting the page. Will stop for now.

Thursday...

Now I shall finish.

The Storm of 1900—Emelise's Tale (Part Three)

I grabbed one of my brother's arms and pulled him towards me. Samuel, I think it was. But I could not see. He coughed up water.

Then I soon found my two other siblings. Again I instructed them to grab onto my dress and not *let go. I forced my way to the door, the wind trying to blow me back.*

Stepping outside onto the underwater porch, the rain pelting my skin, I wanted to stay in the safety of my home. But I knew it would not remain safe for long.

A and S began to complain about how much the rain felt like nails. I could not disagree. I bit my tongue to hold back the tears.

We waded through the deep water with much difficulty. The wind blew so hard, trying to push us back into the house that I knew would soon collapse. My brothers grasped my dress tightly. Our legs almost flew out from under us from the pressure of the current.

But nothing can compare to how cold the water was. Surely the water had come from the Antarctic Ocean itself. My legs turned numb immediately, and I bet you our lips turned blue. My teeth chattered, though I could not hear it due to the howling wind. But I could hear the glass shattering and foundations cracking. How I did not want to move from my spot in the water.

I slowly put one foot in front of the other, my brothers trailing behind me. The water pushed past my dress. I knew that if I fell…if I lost my footing…I would drown. My heavy skirt would carry me under the water and I would not be able to resurface.

I tried not to think about dying and started wading through the water, down the porch steps and into our yard. The water went up to my chest. A's and S's heads bobbed in the water. I tried not to let them go under. Nathan had fear in his eyes, I saw that.

The current drifted us quickly to Mrs. Sealy's house (I actually saw it still standing, thank God). Nathan, Anthony, and Samuel continued to hold onto my dress. One time Samuel's head went under the water, but I pulled it back up.

I reached out for the tree in Mrs. Sealy's yard. The current continued to drift us farther away. I thought I would not be able to grab onto it, but my fingers curled around a branch. My arms ached. N, A, and S pulled me down into the water. I gasped for air.

But, thankfully, Nathan managed to grasp a branch as well, and he helped me pull the boys out of the currents main path.

We again waded through the water towards Mrs. Sealy's front door. I could barely move my legs. They felt so frozen. My fingers were pale.

As the wind blew, the rain hammering on our skin likes nails, I pounded on Mrs. Sealy's door, praying she would answer.

She didn't. I opened the door myself and fell to the floor, water pouring into the house.

"Hurry!" I shouted to my brothers. "Follow me."

I couldn't see. I felt around for my surroundings. A chair...a sofa...a table...stairs!

"Up the stairs!" I instructed. We ran up them as quickly as anyone can do anything and entered a bedroom. We cowered in the corner, hugging each other tightly and shivering so hard, for we were very cold. Nathan prayed out loud, but I fear he did not do so for long. Something in the dark struck him and he went mute.

"Nathan!" I called. No answer.

"Emmie, I'm scared," Samuel shouted above the noise. I could not disagree with him.

"Just stay close," I said.

And we sat there, huddled in the corner in complete darkness. One of my brothers did not answer my cries and the other two wept uncontrollably, frightened.

This house proved to be much safer than ours, for neither the roof nor the foundation shook as much. But I could not help thinking at that moment of Mrs. Sealy. Where was she? Dead? I hoped not.

Hours passed by. My fears increased during those long moments. I felt like a child. A toddler. I wanted my parents. Tears streamed down my face as I whispered the Christmas hymn Silent Night, Holy Night.

Then the silence did come. Oh, the silence. How strange it seemed. No wind. No rain. Just absolute silence. I peeked out the broken window above us and saw the sun rising over the distance. It looked the same as it had That Morning. The exact same. I hated it. I despised it. It looked ugly and deceitful. The sun was betraying me, trying to convince me everything was going to be fine and beautiful, but I knew disaster awaited.

Anthony and Samuel had fallen asleep. I gently moved away from them and examined Nathan. Blood ran down the side of his head. He did not move.

"Nathan?" I whispered. "The storm's over. It's over. Please wake up."

Nothing.

I began to cry. I had lost my brother. The sweetest, most loving brother God had created had died in a hurricane that no one had seen coming. Why?

Anthony and Samuel woke up and immediately asked what had happened and was the storm done? But when they saw Nathan they shushed up. Not even a peppermint stick could have quieted them like the site of Nathan did.

"Is he…?" Anthony asked.

I did not answer. I only gathered up my little brothers and made them start walking down the stairs. The house had withheld the storm. Everything in it was broken, of course, but at least the roof and foundation were still fine.

Slowly walking to the front door, I wondered what I would see when I opened it. Thoughts came flooding into my mind.

I opened the door and froze. My heart stopped. Practically every house was destroyed. Water filled the streets.

But it was when we saw the body on Mrs. Sealy's front porch did A and S go into shock. They gasped, then did not speak. The body was of that man that had helped us before the main part of the storm had arrived, when we had tried to make it to the Tremont Opera House. His face was pale, stomach bloated, and his clothes almost disintegrated, as if the water had melted it.

I hurried A and S past the man and had them sit on the sidewalk.

"Stay here," I said. I then glanced up and saw our house. Our Carson Candy Cane house. It was destroyed. All of it. The roof had been lifted off and probably thrown halfway across the town. The foundation, broken.

"Oh, no," I gasped. But I did not think about that for long. I ran back into Mrs. Sealy's house, up the stairs, and to Nathan. I wept at the sight of his handsome face covered in blood.

"God, why did You let this happen?" I shouted to the sky. "Why Nathan? Why Nathan?" I could no longer go on. I wanted to die right then and there. The entire city of Galveston was destroyed in a disaster hurricane, only God knew where my parents were, not to mention Alice and Edward and how they had fared. My two little brothers were in shock, and the sweetest brother in the world had died. Just kill me now, *I thought.*

But God didn't answer my suicidal plea. Instead, he made Nathan open his eyes.

"Nathan?" I questioned. "Nathan!" I hugged him tightly. But Nathan made no reply. He did not move, did not blink, did not speak. He had gone into shock just as A and S had. God might as well have not answered my prayers. He had burdened me with more work to yet take care of another brother. Yes, I was thankful, but couldn't He have awoken Nathan fully?

I made Nathan stand, and he leaned on my shoulder, practically making me fall over onto the floor because of his great weight over my little strength.

Once outside, I made him sit next to my other unresponsive brothers I started walking over to my Candy Cane house. Oh, how destroyed it was. More like walking on piles of broken lumber than a once glamorous white and red house that had had electricity and chandeliers and a golden harp. Oh, God, why?

Then I saw it. My diary. Oh, how happy I was when I saw that little book. My little book. Hidden under some rubble. How come God had allowed this book to survive but not all the residents of Galveston?

I hugged it close to me, then walked back to my brothers and sat near them. I watched the people stumble past me. I listened to the wailing mothers calling out for their missing children. I sensed the presence of the dead surrounding me as if I had entered an uncovered graveyard with the corpses scattered about.

I looked at the destroyed town. I looked at our no-longer-there Candy Cane house. I looked at my unresponsive brothers. I wept. The tears left trails on my dusty cheeks. I cried for my brothers and sister, for my parents, for the town, and for the dead. And for all the other children who had to experience the sight of seeing a dead body and for those little children who would no longer have parents or siblings.

And I prayed. And wondered why an All Merciful, All Loving *God had allowed such disaster to be bestowed upon us.*

And I cried.

Friday, September 14, 1900

I cannot stop worrying about Alice. Where is she? Why has she not sent word of her survival? What if…

No. I will not think of such thoughts.

My eyes water because of the stench of burning bodies in the air. There is a death toll of 6,000 people.
6,000 people are dead.
They say it may even reach up to 12,000 because so many are missing and who knows if they will be found.
The paper says more. It says the entire island of Galveston was covered with 15.7 feet of water, beating the previous record from the 1875 storm which was only 8 feet.
The anemometer (something that measures wind) at the weather station blew away when the wind speed reached 100 miles an hour. They say at its highest point it was 130 miles per hour.

Saturday, September 15, 1900

Has it really been a week since the hurricane? It feels like just yesterday.

I don't know if I can go on living now. I know I have said that before, but this is different. I have seen the truth. I am no longer hoping. I know.
Picked up a newspaper again. How I dreaded reading it, but it occupied my mind.
I scanned through the *Confirmed Dead* list. So many names. Some I knew. Some not.
Then I saw it. How my heart stopped. My eyes blurred with tears. I could not speak. This is what the newspaper said under the *Confirmed Dead:*

CAROU, Mrs. Jeanie.
CARREN, Mrs. Eugenie
CARRIGAN, Joseph
CARSON, Edward L.
CARTER, A.J.

I needed to do a double-take before I realized. My brother Edward was on the *Confirmed Dead* list. He had been killed in the Storm of 1900. I didn't want to believe it. I tried not to. I said to myself, *It's just another Edward L. Carson. There must be many here in Galveston. It isn't my brother. It isn't.*

But deep down inside I knew the truth. Edward was dead. Plain as day. My stupid, stubborn, mean, teased-me-until-I-hated-him, brother was dead.

I knew what I had to do. I needed to see him. I needed to know for sure that he had died, no questions asked. I would have to go to a morgue. The newspaper said all those names were at the north side of the Strand (whatever that was) between 21st and 22nd street in a temporary morgue.

I am leaving now. It isn't too far away from us. N, A, and S will come with me, but they will not come inside. I worry over what I will see.

I fear I shall never be the same over what I saw in that temporary morgue.

Leaving N, A, and S outside of the building, I silently prayed that maybe Edward was not dead, and he had made it to Little Rock just as I knew he had gone instead of taking those exams.

The dead laid in rows, stretching from wall to wall. Men and women slowly moved though the lines, as if hunting for priceless jewels. Some bodies were uncovered; others had a white sheet blanketed over them. The smell of burnt bodies, ashes, salt water, vomit, and rotting skin penetrated the air.

A woman wearing a white dress walked over towards me. Her eyes were red from crying. How could she bear even the *idea* of having to identify all those bodies?

"May I help you?" she asked in a very high-pitched voice.

I held up the newspaper with my brother's name printed there as if he had won a prize in a fair. "I'm looking for someone. Edward L. Carson. Is he here?" How I hoped he wasn't. How I hoped he had somehow gotten to Little Rock and now sat chatting with Ruth Henry. But I only hoped. All anyone can do these days is hope.

"Come with me. He is over here." The dreaded words.

I followed, stepping over bodies along the way. I saw two boys lying next to each other. They appeared to be twins. One, I could tell, had a broken neck. The other had his brow furrowed and a frown upon his lips. It almost seemed as if he was glaring at his identical brother.

"Do you want to be alone, miss?"

I hadn't even realized we had reached my apparent brother. There was a body before my eyes, covered up in a white sheet though so I could not see exactly who it was.

"We found his name in his jacket pocket." She glanced at me. "I'll leave you by yourself."

But I didn't want to be by myself. I wanted to be with someone I knew. I wanted…

How I wanted everything I wished for.

Taking a deep breath, I fingered the sheet covering this person. I didn't pay any heed to the other bodies surrounding me. I only watched this one.

Then I closed my eyes and pulled back the sheet, revealing the head of a dark brown-haired young man. His nose was pointy. His jaw set as if angry. I cried out. This was my brother. Edward. Oh, God, why? I couldn't stop staring, though I knew I shouldn't or I would pay with nightmares. His face was so pale and…decomposed. Almost as if the water had melted his skin right off.

I pulled the sheet down more so I could check his jacket pockets for anything of value or remembrance. Tears trailed down my cheeks. My nose ran. I believe I have cried more in these last few days than I have in my life.

My fingers rapped around something in his vest. I pulled it out. His golden pocket watch. The one he had received on his thirteenth birthday with the words, *To my son, Edward Lawrence, on your birthday. With much love, Father* engraved on the top. I clicked it open. The hands did not move.

With tears streaming down my cheeks and memories flashing, I took out everything else he had in his pockets. Some shriveled up pieces of paper (I could not read what they said) and an envelope. I gingerly opened up the envelope marked *Edward Lawrence Carson.* Found lots cash inside. Probably $30 or more. Oh, Edward. Had he earned all that money from clam catching? And then I saw it. A picture. A picture of Ruth Henry was tucked in-between the bills. The water had stained and discolored it, but I could still plainly make out Miss Ruth Henry, prettiest brown haired, green eyed young lady in all of Arkansas.

A thought came to me as I stared at that picture. I needed to contact Ruth. After all, the two were planning to marry. I dreaded the thought of telling her.

Then I returned the money, picture, and unreadable papers to Edward. I didn't want those things. They were Edward's, not mine. And now he was dead. I guess I figured it would bring me bad luck.

But I did keep the pocket watch. Somehow when I traced my finger over Edward's name it comforted me.

I walked out. I am going to return tomorrow for Edward's body. He deserves a proper burial. Maybe I can find a priest to say the benediction. Some men will have to help me dig the hole for him, for I have no intention of having him burned as the rest of the bodies have been.

N, A, and S had a hard time accepting Edward's death. I had an even harder time telling them.

Here is a copy of my letter to Ruth H:

> *September 15, 1900*
> *Dear Ruth,*
>> *I know you have probably heard some gruesome stories of the disaster that struck Galveston, Texas, on Saturday, September 8. Let me tell you: They are all true. What people say about the bodies littering the streets is real, though I wish it were not.*
>> *Nathan, Anthony, and Samuel are alive. My brothers suffered a few days of shock, but they eventually awoke. However, I fear Nathan was struck by something during the storm and he is now completely blind.*
>> *Mother and Papa are not here with us. I do not know where they are. I have received no word from my sister Alice either.*
>> *The real reason I am writing you, Ruth, is because Edward's name was in the newspaper under* Confirmed Dead. *I went to the morgue to see him myself. I identified him. He is really dead, Ruth.*
>> *I am sorry to bring you such grave news. I am sorry your future together will not take place as planned. I am sorry you will not marry my brother. I am sorry he is dead, but I knew you had to know.*
>>> *Your friend,*
>>>> *Emelise Carson*

Also wrote Kate a letter, though I will not copy it here, for my hand hurts from writing.

Ha. What a funny thing to say in a time like this. My hand hurts from writing. What a little pain compared to the large one I am undergoing inside of me.

Sunday, September 16, 1900

Edward will not receive a proper burial. Neither will those twins boys, nor the other hundred bodies in that morgue. The Dead Gangs came and gathered them all up last night, then took them to the large fires growing throughout town to burn them. The woman there gave me the news this morning when I came to take Edward.

I am having a hard time trying to imagine the horror that happened to my own brother. How did Edward fair, being thrown into a large bonfire? Did his arms flail out as I had seen one body do? Or did he just simply lay there on top the rest of the bodies, unmoving as the sea of orange consumed him?

Is there even a God out there anymore? Why does he not answer my prayers? Why does he allow me to suffer so?

Nathan does not cry as much anymore. Instead, he whispers. "I will never play the piano, never play the harp, never help with the dishes, never see the flowers, never see anything anymore."

I try to tell him that that is not so, that he can still imagine them as he did before. But he turns away. I miss my kind, understanding brother.

They say bad news comes in threes. And it has. How much does this All Merciful God think I can take?

I saw William Murney walking through the streets at evening time. My dear friend William. My first friend. He had survived! I thought this day would turn out to be a good one, but it hasn't; not after what he told me.

I ran towards him and hugged him tightly, not caring that we had met only once and it was probably improper for a young girl to hug a boy. But I didn't care, and it seemed neither did William. He hugged me back and cried softly.

"What happened?" I asked. "Where are the other children?"

He only shook his head. I grabbed his hand and pulled him over to the sidewalk, motioning him to sit and tell me the story.

It took him a while, but he finally began talking. How I did not want to listen when I heard what he had to say.

"It was late Saturday afternoon before the Sisters realized something was wrong. Sister Elizabeth had gone into town to get some food so we could have supper, and the others deeply worried about her getting caught in the storm.

"The Sisters gathered us together and moved us into the stronger girls' dorm. Some of us could tell this was not an ordinary storm because the Sisters *never* brought the boys into the girls' dorm.

"All ninety of us children huddled on the second floor of that dorm, listening to the rain and hearing the waves crash into the boys' dorm.

"We were frightened," William explained, tears streaming down his face. "I held my little brother close and whispered that everything would be all right. But I wasn't so sure myself.

"Then we heard the boys' dorm collapse. We all imagined it being drifted out to sea, and the little ones began to scream with fear. It was your sister Alice, Emelise, who started to sing the old French hymn 'Queen of the Waves' to help calm us. She sounded so lovely; no one could resist singing along. Our voices rose over the pounding of the rain and we could hear nothing from the outside world."

Tears came flooding in my eyes. How brave of my sister. I remember her singing parts of that song to us when she came to visit a few weeks ago. I can still recall the first verse. *Queen of the Waves, look forth across the ocean from north to south from east to stormy west. See how the waters with tumultuous motion rise up and foam without a pause or rest...*

William continued, "The Sisters told one of our workers, Henry, to collect clothesline rope. They began to tie the clothesline to the cinctures around their waist, and then to the children. Each Sister had six to eight orphans tied around her waist so 'we all stay together.' I remember one of the Sisters holding two of the smallest children in her arms, promising she would never let go.

"The windows began to break from the ferocious wind. Some of the glass injured the children.

"We older ones began to kneel and pray aloud, asking the Lord to protect Sister Elizabeth and to protect us."

The boy paused for a moment, overcome with emotion. Then he proceeded. "We heard water rush into the girls' dorm right below us. The children began to scream again, and once more your sister sang 'Queen of the Waves.'

"But then some of the children, including myself, looked out the broken windows in time to see a large ship come crashing directly into us, Emelise. It hit the orphanage so hard, all ninety of us toppled to the floor. The orphanage was then lifted off its foundation and dragged into the menacing ocean.

"I cannot forget that feeling, Emelise," William said. "I was so scared. The Sisters were unbelievably brave, however. They continued to sing 'Queen of the Waves' until the roof caved in, trapping us all. I grabbed my little brother tightly, trying to keep his head above the water. But then a beam or something hit me and..." William paused, wiping away the tears. "I never saw my brother again."

I hugged William as he cried softly. I told him that my older brother had died as well, so I knew how he felt.

"But that's not all, Emelise," he said, pulling away. "I remember being in the cold water. Remember trying to stay alive. But I can't recall anything else, and the next thing I knew, I was alive and in a tree, three of my orphanage friends, Albert and Frank, clinging to it next to me.

"When I was hanging onto that floating tree, I saw a ways off some of the Sisters sprawled out on the sand or debris. They were dead, the orphans still tied to their waist."

I could not believe it. Did not want to. "All of the Sisters? And the children?"

William glanced away. "Only Albert, Frank, and I survived, Emelise." I did not want to think about little Anna May, the girl who had begged me to come see her, no longer in this world. And what of Sarah, the girl who had a crush on Nathan?

Then William looked me right in the eye and said, "I saw your sister, too. She was lying on top of some wood, four orphans scattered next to her and..."

I stopped listening after that. I grew numb again. I did not even cry. I slightly heard William say some fisherman had come and rescued them, and that he was staying at St. Mary's Infirmary and helping the Sisters there. But I did not respond, even when he asked if he could do anything for me.

Alice. My sister... The sweetest sister in the world...swallowed by a watery grave? I did not want to believe it. I wanted to keep imagining her running up the sidewalk towards me, calling out "Emelise, Emelise! How I missed you!" But I saw no one and heard no voice.

My sister is dead, dear diary. Why does God mock me so? Does he not even care?

I have not cried. I am all cried out over Edward that I do not even have any tears left for my sister. And what of my parents? Is God going to torture me and confirm them gone, too?

A and S cry, though I do not. They keep wailing, "We want Alice! We want Mother and Papa! We want our other rabbits! We want Edward and Nathan back!"

    I explained to them that Alice and Edward are in Heaven with Jesus, and that Mother and Papa will come back, and Nathan is still here.

    "But Nathan's not the same!"

    How I know.

Monday, September 17, 1900

The Red Cross is here. They have arrived with food and tents and water and medicine. They set themselves up not too far from us, the yellow tents sticking out like a red licorice whip in a jar of black ones. I think I am going to take Nathan, Anthony, and Samuel over for a look-see.

Some extraordinary news, dear diary, though I am trying not to be too happy about it because it just makes my heart yearn for Alice. I almost feel as though I am betraying her because I am not mourning like I probably should.

    I gathered my brothers up and started to walk over to the Red Cross camps, a large line of people already forming. We stood behind a woman and her small daughter, waiting our turn. I couldn't help staring at the girl. She was as limp as a doll in her mother's arms. I think she was dead.

    The line moved slowly. A and S grew tired of standing and plopped onto the ground. Nathan hugged my arm tightly, practically cutting off the circulation. His eyes darted around. I have never seen him so frightened of the world.

When it was *finally* our turn, a lady in a white dress ushered us over to a certain yellow tent used as the medical station. She examined my eyes, and then my little brothers'. When she tried to shine the light in Nathan's eyes, he shouted out, "Don't! I can't see anything!"

The nurse glanced my way worriedly, then forced a smile on her face and said, "You are perfectly fit, young man."

"No," Nathan muttered. "I'm not."

My face grew red with embarrassment. I quickly asked where we could get some food.

The nurse looked me up and down. "You could definitely use some, I dare say. I can practically see your bones through your dress."

I blushed. I hadn't noticed how skinny I was getting.

Once told, we walked over to the food tent where, yet again, there was another line. Not one person spoke the entire time. It was deadly silent; the only sound made by the Red Cross volunteers as they scraped the soup ladles against the great kettles.

N, A, S, and I took our soup and piece of bread each slightly far away from the camp. We sat on the ground and began eating.

Soon after we had started, I heard a voice in front of me say, "Don't you say grace before a meal?"

I jumped, my soup splashing onto my dress. An old woman stood before me with brown hair and a simple dress. She had the Red Cross symbol pinned to her bodice.

"Well?" she asked again. "Don't you?"

"I used to," I stuttered. "But not anymore. What do I have to be thankful for?"

She knelt down on the ground with us. Her eyes were kind. "You have your brothers here, I see. Shouldn't you thank Him for that?"

Anthony shouted out, "But not our parents! And not Alice or Edward, either."

The old woman reached over and hugged Anthony. He did not resist as I thought he would. Who was this stranger who wanted to talk to us about thanking God and started hugging my brother?

She then made us introduce ourselves and tell our story. I didn't want to, but how could I resist?

So I told her our names, about Alice and Edward, and how our parents are missing.

She then embraced all of us at the same time. "How truly sad. My name is Clara Barton. I am here to help you find your parents."

Clara Barton! As in, the Red Cross founder? I was speechless. Clara Barton had traveled all the way to the island of Galveston just to assist us in our dire need?

"Now, we can put a notice in the newspaper and around town to help you find your parents. When was the last time you saw them?" C.B talked as though Mother and Papa would be found tomorrow.

Anthony and Samuel began to hop up and down, exclaiming, "We're gonna find Mother! We're gonna find Papa!"

C.B hugged them again. "We certainly are." I liked how she assured us so much, and helped us, but I wished she would have not gotten my little brothers hopes up so much. What if our parents cannot be found? What if they—dare I say it—died in the hurricane as 6,000 others did?

They are having Masses throughout Galveston, though it is Monday. People set up chairs and there is even Communion if you go to a Catholic "church."

Nathan wanted to attend, but I said no. He asked why.

"Because we have *nothing* to be thankful for," I insisted.

"You're alive, aren't you?" Nathan asked. "Isn't that something to be thankful for?"

Where did this sudden boost of energy come from? Hadn't he *just* disagreed with the nurse and claimed he was not *perfectly fit*?

"But should we be thankful for the fact that Edward and Alice are dead and that our parents are missing?"

Nathan did not answer my question. He only said, "I'm going. You can either take me there or let me find it on my own." He started to walk off. Stubborn brother! Anthony and Samuel squealed, "I want to go to church, too!" SIGH.

So we went. People sat in chairs around a table used as the altar. We sang familiar hymns like "Amazing Grace" and "The Blood of Jesus." I despised all of it. I didn't want to sing, but when Nathan nudged me, how could I not? How could these people even think of praising God when they had lost so much?

I was thankful when church service ended.

Tuesday, September 18, 1900

Construction has already begun on some of the buildings. Muscular men gather usable wood and throw it into a pile. The stuff they do not want, they burn it along with the bodies. Along with Edward. I wonder, was Alice burned or were the people who found her kind enough to bury a soon-to-be Catholic Sister?

Wednesday, September 19, 1900

C.B sure did do a good job of putting notices around Galveston! Practically on every telephone pole or building there is a note for Mr. and Mrs. James Carson from their children. My hopes are now rising. I think we will find our parents soon.

I rescued someone!

I decided walk around used-to-be-Galveston to take my mind off some things and *maybe* catch sight of my parents if I was lucky.

How ugly everything looked. The heat wasn't as bad as it was before That Day, thankfully. Whenever a fire came into my view, I turned away. You cannot imagine it, dear diary. The sight of those bodies burning… How long will it go on? I heard the Dead Gangs are making men do this job at *gunpoint* because no one wants to.

Anyway, I just happened to be walking by this one house when I heard a sound.

I stopped and listened. Then I heard it again.

"Help." Those words ever so quietly. I thought for sure I had imagined it.

"Please help."

"Where are you?"

"Here."

I turned around. The sound was coming from *under* that house. I began to pull boards away. Then I saw it. A hand. I shrieked. But then the hand moved, and the voice spoke again, pleading for help.

After what seemed like forever, I had managed to pull away enough wood to see a young girl, not much older than six, lying on the dirt. Her lips were extremely parched, her dress torn, and she looked to be as skinny as a rail.

Once I had made a hole large enough for her to crawl out, she didn't seem to want to move. Only then did I realize she *couldn't* move. I grabbed her one fragile arm (the other one I could not reach and she was grasping something, though I could not tell what) and gently pulled her out, me then toppling over onto the pavement with exhaustion.

I hovered over her. "Are you all right?"

She didn't answer me, but, instead continued to cling to the object she held in her one hand. I examined it closely. It was a picture frame, battered and dirty, with a picture inside. The glass was broken, but I could clearly make out the little girl in the image along with her parents, I suspected. Where were they now? Dead? Looking for their daughter?

I called for help. A man came running over, gathered up the girl, and carried her to a nearby Red Cross camp. I followed.

I sat outside of the medical tent, waiting for news. Finally a nurse came out and sat next to me.

"She's going to be fine."

I sighed with relief. "What happened to her? How could she have lived so long under the rubble?"

"My guess is that she had some access to water while being trapped. That kept her alive. She is very, very lucky you came along."

"How come she couldn't move?"

"Lack of exercise, oxygen, food, and water. She was also in a very tight spot, which made her legs and arms crammed into that position. Don't worry, though. We think she will be her fine self before long. We're trying to figure out her name so we can see if she has any living family members."

What are the odds that I would have happened to walk by that house at that exact moment? Maybe…there is a God who cares enough to keep that little girl alive and allow me to rescue her.

I have been thinking of that crazy family that came to us before the worst of the storm. The Mr. and Mrs. and little boy. Did the boy die after being struck by his father's briefcase? Did the parents die?

Next Day...

I am now sitting in one of the tents in the Red Cross camp. C.B came and spoke with me, trying to reassure me that the newspaper is always wrong, but I am not so sure.

Our parents. Our parents were in the newspaper. Under the *Feared Dead* column. When I saw that I didn't speak. I was so shocked. I didn't cry either, for I was all cried out long ago.

As soon as I read *CARSON, James* and *CARSON, Lillian,* I threw down the paper, gathered up my brothers, and marched over to the RC camps to find Clara Barton. She didn't trust me at first, I don't think. She only smiled, saying I must be mistaken. I assured her I was not and even told her to find a newspaper and check herself. She walked away and after a few minutes came back to us, grim-faced.

"You children will stay here from now on until we find your parents. They're alive; don't you worry. You can stay in a tent next to me. Come along."

I stuttered a reply. "They're dead!"

She turned around. "No. I don't believe they are."

I didn't want to continue to talk back to an older woman, so I grabbed my three brothers by the arm and pulled them along.

So now I am sitting on one of our two make-shift beds. The tent is small, but it will do until, as C.B said, "We find your parents."

I wish she would stop trying to encourage us. It will only make everything worse when A and S find out the *real* truth. Nathan figured it out, I can tell, but it is that C.B. I just wish she would stop saying, "They're alive; don't worry.

We'll find them." A and S hang onto that thread of hope, but I do not. I am not even very sad. I figured it would come to this long ago. We are orphans.

Thursday, September 20, 1900

C.B does not listen to me. Every minute of the day she speaks with A and S about finding our parents. They smile and nod, asking how *soon* will they be here. She tells them very soon, very soon indeed. Does she know something I do not? Or is she just simply saying that to comfort them? I wish she would stop. I no longer look up to her as the *amazing Red Cross founder*. I am starting to despise her.

Took a walk to clear my mind and get away from C.B. It hasn't quite registered that we are orphans, though I knew it many days ago Just didn't want to admit it, not even here in my private diary. How will A and S take it? They cried a river over Edward and Alice each. What will their reaction be when I tell them their parents—both of them—died just as their siblings did? And that a Merciful God took them away from us? And that we are orphans and will be soon sent to an orphanage? Maybe even separated?

I have made up my mind. No longer will C.B keep the hopes of finding our parents alive to A and S. I shall tell them tomorrow morning, before they go to church services with C.B (yes, she has starting taking them, saying we should thank God for all he has done for us).

It's late. My stomach is churning with just the *idea* of having to tell my six and eight year old brothers. My little brothers who sleep with their one surviving rabbit and whisper bedtime prayers to it. My brothers who still have those red handkerchiefs tied around their necks so they can "look like twins." My brothers who call each other *Herby* and *Curt* because they are two peas in a pod. How am I going to tell them?

It is now morning, next day. C.B and my brothers left to one of the many church services scattered around Galveston.

    I told my brothers. I don't think they believed me.

    Soon after I woke up, my brothers did, shouting, "Let's go find Miss Clara!" and gathered up their white rabbit.

    I stopped them.

    "We need to talk," I said. "Sit down, Anthony and Samuel."

    "But Miss Clara is expecting us!"

    "That can wait. Now sit."

    They did so, but with much grumbling.

    "Now," I started, "you know how Miss Clara has been telling you Mother and Papa are alive? Well…" I paused, then continued. "Mother and Papa are not coming back, Anthony, Samuel. They are in Heaven with Jesus, just like Edward and Alice are."

    Anthony immediately started to protest. "Nu-huh! Miss Clara says they are coming back and that they will be here any day to take us home!"

    I took a deep breath to calm myself. "Miss Clara is wrong. They are not coming back. They never are coming back."

    Speaking of you-know-who, C.B barged into the tent at that exact moment. She twirled around—even with her being in her eighties—and sang out, "Good morning, children! Are you ready for church services?"

Anthony stood up and hugged C.B. "Is Emelise right?" he asked. "Are Mother and Papa dead?"

C.B was downright shocked. She looked at me. "Where in heavens name did you get such an idea?"

"Then it's not true?" A asked, hopeful.

"Of course not! You listen to me: we are going to find you parents even if it takes me a year. Now come along, before we are late for church services."

A and S followed the old woman, as if they were glued to her. But before he was completely out of the tent, A stuck his tongue out at me, as if to say, *I told you so.* I think my brother is getting back to his old self, and I am happy for that, but I wish he would take me more seriously. I wish he would believe me. What's going to happen when my parents' names show up in the *Confirmed Dead* section of the newspaper? Is C.B still going to say they are alive and well and we will find them?

Afternoon same day...

Isabelle is no longer here. I went to see her today and the nurse told me her parents had arrived late yesterday night. Isabelle was feeling some better, and when she saw them she perked right up and wanted to go home. So her parents left with her.

I wish I could have said goodbye.

The Clines are here! I saw them walking through the streets towards my direction. Esther saw me and started to run. Then she hugged me tightly and said, "We still can't find Mama! Where is she?" It seems they hang onto the same hope of their parent being alive that my brothers do. Allie May spoke with me some, asking who was alive and how I was doing.

"Fine," I said. Fine? I am not fine. "And you?"

"Papa went back to work the other day, but he still looks for Mama. He checks the paper every day." Then she gave me a serious look. "Everyone blames my father for the hurricane. But it was not his fault. How could he have known?" She stopped talking and stared at me wide-eyed. "*You* think it's his fault, too!"

I stuttered a "No I don't." But really I do think it was his fault. No, I *know* it was his fault. I don't think I shall ever forgive him for the despair he has caused me.

Friday, September 21, 1900

The Red Cross nurse who spoke with me about Isabelle asked me for assistance in the medical tent! I am now a volunteer for the Red Cross, tending the wounded and feeding the hungry.

My first *patient* was a sixteen year old boy named Vincent. He had light brown hair and ocean blue eyes. I think he looks a bit like Nathan. Handsome.

He only had a slight wound on his cheek that needed eleven stitches. He just chatted away while I stitched him up, not flinching one bit. I found out he has a sister living in Massachusetts, another one in Connecticut, and two brothers in Maryland. All are married and have children!

I asked where his parents were. A mistake.

"They died in the hurricane just like everyone else did." I thought I saw a tear forming in his eye. I blushed in embarrassment and apologized.

"No need. You were just making polite conversation." He's also just as kind as Nathan, if I might add.

Then he hopped off the examination table and walked out of the tent. His head popped back in. "Maybe I'll see you around, Miss Emelise." Then he was gone. Miss Emelise. I like that. It makes me sound so grown up.

I just thought I would add this bit in. As I was walking towards the food tent for a lunch meal, I caught sight of a woman. She was completely scratched up and dirty, so much that I am sure no one knew who she was, even if it had been the president's wife herself.

    I caught her staring at me out of the corner of my eye. I turned. She was a few yards away, but I could easily tell she had a look of shock on her face. She took one step forward, as if she was going to come near me. But I hurried away, not turning back. Why did that woman stare at me so? I did not know her, but by the looks of her face it appeared she knew me. She must have mistaken me for someone else.

Saturday, September 22, 1900

Considering the fact that I volunteer at the Red Cross camp practically all day every day, and I cannot watch my brothers, I suppose I should thank C.B. She plays with my little brothers and takes them to church services and with Nathan she makes him feel useful by having him help with serving food and such.

    But I will not thank her. At least not yet. Not when I still have so much on my mind and I hear my brothers—even Nathan now—say our parents are alive and why don't you believe, Emelise? Because it is not true. Because I know it is not true. We are orphans.

    I do not cry at night, though, over this horrible fortune that was destined upon me. I only think. And wonder why.

Evening.

Had another interesting patient today. An old man. He spoke of his dog, Marion, who had saved him during the hurricane. To make a long story short—since I am quite tired—the man had been trapped under the rubble of his house and was going to soon die of dehydration when Marion happened to sniff him out and continued to bark uncontrollably until rescuers responded to the call.

Next Day...

C.B took me to church services, even though I did not want to go. The singing is much more different than before the hurricane. It almost seems...dead. Pleading, more like. Pleading to God.

And the people cry during the service. They say, "Amen!" when the preacher says something encouraging.

Then I saw Vincent! He was sitting a few rows in front of me. When he turned around, he nodded his greeting.

Once the church service was over, I ran up to him.

"Top o' the mornin' to ya, Em," he said.

I laughed. Then he asked if I would like to take a walk around Galveston for a bit. C.B agreed to let me go. I almost glared at her then. She sounded a bit like my mother, giving me permission when asked. I hated it, but followed Vincent.

We walked randomly around, chatting as if we were old friends. My shyness must have washed away like the town. I did blush occasionally when he would turn and grin at me.

And already he calls me Em! He *insisted* I call him Vince "or else!"

Then as we perambulated back towards the Red Cross camp, he asked me to tell him about *my* family. I struggled with the words when I told him about Edward and Alice, but I did not hold back. I felt like I could talk to him like I could talk to Alice or Nathan.

When I spoke of my parents and us now being orphans, he stopped dead in his tracks. His eyes watered and he mumbled condolences. I told him how Clara Barton continues to tell my brothers they are alive, when I know deep down they are not. He surprised me then by saying, "Don't give up hope yet, Em. You never know what tomorrow will bring."

We were silent the rest of the way back. I thought of Vince's quote. Why had he said that to me? Were my parents alive? Or did he simply just want to comfort me? Or was he being the same old rascal Vince and he was only saying random thoughts?

We said our goodbyes in front of my tent. As I turned around I heard him call, "See ya later, Em."

Another friend since William!

I walked into my tent and grabbed the hand mirror I had found the other day. My face has purple scars over it, my hair is literally a rat's nest, and my dress is caked with mud and torn. My hands are not smooth and soft like they used to, and my fingernails are broken with half-moons of brown. I am as ugly as a crow.

Monday, September 24, 1900

My brain is still processing the meaning of Vince's quote. But I still cannot comprehend the definition of it. Are my parents alive after all? I wonder that numerous times.

Nathan and Anthony and Samuel seem to think so. Nathan believed me at first, that they are dead, but after some convincing from C.B, his confidence changed. His mood has changed as well. He seems to be enjoying his time with the old woman. He does not cry at night over his complete blindness, but, instead, turns his attention to *me* and trying to comfort *me* because I truly do believe we are orphans, though everyone tells me otherwise. I wish to ask them, how do you know? Have you personally seen James and Lillian Carson alive and well? Did they speak and ask for their children? Where are they?

I receive no answer to the silent questions tumbling in my brain.

When I wrote my last entry, I had not yet walked out of my tent for the morning. But now that I have become acquainted with C.B and my brothers this day, it seems as though they…sense something I do not. C.B especially. She told me, right when she saw me, that she *knew* our parents would show up any day now, A and S agreeing with her. But how do they know? I fear A and S will be heartbroken by the plain comprehension that they are orphans.

I fear *I* shall forever be dull and silent, never once again participating in the games and activities as I did before this unbearable news hit me.

And I still wonder why. Why, God, why?

Friday, September 28, 1900

How does one begin writing about the events that have taken place over these past few days? How does one describe the *feelings* the characters of my life felt?

I shall try to tell you, dear diary.

After I finished my last entry on Monday, I hurried to the medical tent to help with the patients. C.B and my brothers were off somewhere else, to a church service, I believed, even though it was not Sunday.

I was wrapping white cloth around a young boy's head when a nurse came rushing in, calling out, "We need the doctor immediately." The main doctor hurried out, grabbing his bag of medical supplies along the way.

Thinking nothing of it, I continued to wind the bandages around the boy's injured head.

Then I heard it. Faintly, at first, but the voice grew louder. It was what the man was calling out that startled me.

"Edward! Edward!" I heard from the adjacent tent. I did nothing at first, the message still processing.

Then I, too, ran out of that medical tent and into the other one. The doctor was hovering over a severely sick man, trying to test his temperature. But the man continued to shout, "Edward! Edward, come back here!"

I slowly made my way towards the sick male. He was writhing in his bed, his hands tightly grasping the bed sheets. His face was contorted in pain, his clothes soaked in sweat. The woman sitting next to him had her hands covering her face. She was weeping. When she glanced up at me, I realized she was the same woman I had seen the other day, the one who had stopped and stared.

Once she saw me, she stood up and hugged me. She did not hesitate. I almost wanted to shove her away from me. I did not know this woman. Why did it appear to her that I did?

I sniffed. Somehow over the intense stench of dirt and ashes on her clothes, I smelled a familiar smell. Lavender.

I then glanced at the seriously ill man lying on the cot. He had a familiar look to him, but I couldn't place it. I pulled away from the woman's arms and looked at her. Her face was smudged with dirt and smeared with blood. She had brown hair and blue eyes like someone I knew…

"Edward! Edward!" The man continued to call out. I slowly started piecing together the pieces of the puzzle.

Then the woman ran her delicate fingers over my hair. She whispered, "My Emelise. Oh, Emelise."

It clicked.

I embraced my mother fiercely. I thought for sure I would have cracked her in half—she was so thin. But I didn't. And she hugged me back just as tightly.

"Emelise, Emelise. My Emelise," she murmured. The tears came flooding to my eyes.

Turning towards the man on the bed, I took in the familiar features of a man I had known my entire life. Under the layers of dirt and sweat, I saw faded scars. When his eyes opened, I saw they were gray. Even though it was quite messy, his hair was parted over to the side.

I rushed over to him and knelt down, the tears streaming down my cheeks. "Papa, Papa," I said, overcome with emotion. His sweaty head turned my way. He smiled. "Emelise?" he mumbled. "Where have you been?"

All I could think of was this: Clara Barton was right. So were Nathan, Anthony, and Samuel. And Vince. Surely his quote had meant he knew my parents were alive, right?

Oh, how I usually hated it when my brothers were right. But this time I did not care. Really, I was incredibly happy they were right.

We are not orphans.

After I found my brothers and brought them to the tent, they squealed with delight at the sight of their parents. Mother cried. Papa cried, now fully aware of whom these children were. The nurses cried. My brothers and I cried.

Now I will skip to the more important part, since for the first thirty minutes we only hugged and wept.

We sat down, and I told Mother to tell us how she had come to the Red Cross camp and where had she been these past few weeks?

Mother began. "Once we left the house that Saturday for the restaurant, I tried not to think of you children alone in the big house during a storm. But all through dinner, the blowing wind and hammering rain did not subside. James—uh, your father, that is—tried to calm my worries, and we headed to the Tremont Opera House, despite the streets being flooded. Besides, it wasn't that far away from the restaurant we had visited.

"Once we entered the opera house, we found numerous other people huddled in there as well, trying to take shelter during the storm. I couldn't help but think of you children during that moment." Mother paused and stroked Samuel's hair. Then she continued. "We remained in the opera house for a good many hours. Then the lights when out, and everyone began to panic and scream. Some people wished to take chances and try to head to the YMCA, where they said it would be safer. But your father and I decided to stay where we were.

"Then, probably at two in the morning, the opera house began to shake with such ferocity. Like a leaf. I then knew we probably should have left the opera house, for it would no longer be safe.

"Just at that moment, the roof collapsed on us. I remember nothing of that moment except that a searing pain shot through my back. Next thing I knew, the storm was over and I was stranded under feet of rubble."

Tears flooded my mother's eyes as she told us she had been lucky enough not to be completely surrounded by rubble, and had some room to move her arms around. "But I could not get up. So much wood and rocks were stacked on top of my back that I felt like it would crush my lungs and I would suffocate.

"Then I started to hear a sound. When the enveloping dust cleared some, I saw—a few feet away from me—your father trapped just as badly as I. Neither of us could move. We could hardly even turn our heads." Mother told us how she and Papa remained in that position for days until someone cleared enough rubble to get them out. She said it was truly a miracle she had survived, for lack of food and water. "I was extremely tempted to drink the water in the puddles around me. I thought for sure it was salt water. But when I thought I could no longer bear having no water, I drank it. Only I found out the puddle I drank was not salt water, but actually pure rain water. I believe that kept me alive until someone could rescue me."

"Weren't you so, so thirsty?" Samuel asked, eyes wide.

"Very," Mother answered, hugging her son close. "But I only kept praying to God that he would allow me to live so I could try to find you children.

"Once rescued, your father and I were taken to one of the hospitals, where we stayed there for numerous days with severe wounds. I had an injured back that was covered in blood and bruises because of that great weight I had been bearing. Your father had injured his leg terribly, and the doctors were afraid it would have to be amputated. But he recovered, and we were sent out of the hospital because we weren't *as bad* as some of the other people. "Only we were still dazed by what had happened and didn't know where to go. We wandered around the destroyed town of Galveston, looking for you children but trying to not get injured, because we were still not completely well."

"Didn't you see the posts Clara Barton had put around town?" I asked.

"No, Emelise. We didn't. Truth be told, we never even looked in the newspaper for your names, much less read the notices around town. We had read a few, though, once we were released from the hospital, but none of them were from you and I began to lose hope of ever finding you.

"But you were also in the *Feared Dead* column of the newspaper!" I claimed.

"I'm sure we were, Emelise. No one asked for our names. Not one person. When we were at the hospital they were so incredibly busy, I believe no one had time. Their top priority was to get us out of there and make room for more people. Besides, we were alive. They don't put alive people's names in the newspaper, do they? The newspaper journalists probably just figured, since no one had asked our names and a

James and Lillian Carson had not been announced alive yet, we were dead—or feared dead, as you said.

"Then your father began getting extremely exhausted during the day and started complaining about his leg hurting. I feared for the worst. They had taken us out of the hospital way too early. I wanted to find help, but I didn't know where to go. Only when I heard there were Red Cross camps did I head over here.

"One day, I saw you—at least, I thought it was you—walk by and stare at me. I thought for sure you—if it was you—would have recognized me. But when you hurried away did I then realize how truly wretched I looked, which increased my doubts of ever finding you children because you would never have known who I was."

"You mean," Anthony stated, clearly shocked, "I could have walked right by you and I didn't even know it?"

"Yes, Anthony," Mother laughed.

"I would have noticed you if I saw you, Mama," Samuel said, all proud. "But I didn't see you."

Mother laughed again, tears forming in her eyes still. "After that your father only grew worse, so worse that he began to shout out in his delirium. That's when you heard him, Emelise, and, well, you know the rest."

Anthony then turned to me and said, "Ha, Emelise! Told you they were alive. You said they weren't." He stuck out his tongue.

But this time, I didn't stick my tongue back out at him or smirk or roll my eyes. I smiled. My parents are alive.

We remained in the tent for hours, talking and talking. I have not told Mother of the deaths of her two oldest children, yet. This is too happy of a moment to spoil. Tomorrow.

Saturday, September 29, 1900

Something happened last night while I was sleeping. Something overcame me, and I began to cry. The tears slid down the side of my face, touching my ears and wetting the pillow.

Though I have known my parents are alive for numerous days, I never really let it sink in. I no longer need to care for my brothers, worrying over them every minute of every hour of every day, wondering if they will see a horrifying sight and cry in their sleep. I no longer will need to find food for them or help them dress each morning. Or scrub their faces, wiping the tears and grime and blood away. Or sing until they fall asleep at night. *Or worry over them.* I never realized how much I worried over my little brothers. Before this hurricane, I could have cared less about them. I could have cared less about Edward. But now that I know what it feels like to lose a brother, I never want to go through that again.

And I will never have to. My brothers are safe thanks to Clara Barton and the Red Cross and even that man that had helped us before the brunt of the storm came upon us, the man that had been washed up on Mrs. Sealy's doorstep.

Clara Barton. She had been right. She had tried to convince me that she knew my parents were alive, and she sure did convince my brothers, but how did she know? How did she know they weren't lying in a gutter, rotting away, or already burned by the Dead Gangs?

How did Vince know? How did he know I needed that quote at just the right time and how it matched up to these past events?

And just think, dear diary. My future is no longer as easy to read as an open book. We will not leave to an orphanage as I feared and be adopted by some family I would never care about. Instead, it is like a mystery. Who knows what lies around the bend now?

I stay with Papa for hours. He still calls out in his delirium for Edward, but not so often as before. His fever is still raging, though.

     The doctor constantly has a worried look on his face. I heard him talking to one of the nurses. They are worrying about Papa's leg. It seems to be infected.

Saw Vince. Actually, he saw me. He began his greeting as he had last time. "Top o' the mornin' to ya, Em."

     I laughed. "Hello, Vince."

     "How's your father?"

     I paused. "He still has a fever and is delirious."

     "He'll get better soon," Vince insisted.

     "Vince," I asked, "last week, when you said that quote about not knowing what tomorrow will bring, how did you know my parents would show up practically the next day?"

     You know what he told me, dear diary? First he laughed, then said, "I didn't. I was just repeating a quote I had read in a book. Has a little ring to it, don't you think?"

     Vince! I punched him in the arm.

When Clara Barton walked by me, I called out to her. I didn't know how to begin my apology. C.B had repeatedly tried to convince me my parents were alive, and I had hated her for it. She had given my brothers hope—hope I did not believe in.

     "Miss Clara," I started, "I just want to say I am sorry for—"

     "Don't say a thing, Emelise," C.B interrupted. "You were only trying to accept what you thought was the truth. There is no need for an apology."

     "But I want to apologize!" I insisted. "I started to hate you for continuously trying to persuade my brothers."

The old woman hugged me. "I understand completely, Emelise. Please, don't feel upset. Can we be friends and leave it at that?"

I almost cried. She was so understanding.

Monday, October 1, 1900

I told Mother all I had gone through during the weeks they were missing. We both wept when I recalled my encounter with Edward's body and how Alice gave her life to save some of the orphans of St. Mary's Orphan Asylum. Then I told her about Nathan and him becoming completely blind and how I had to take care of my three brothers alone.

"You were very brave, Emelise," my mother said. I remembered weeks before That Day when my mother would only give me insults, and, if a compliment, then it would have a negative edge to it. But there was no negativity in her sentence. Only pride. Was my mother's new attitude towards me different because she had almost lost me? If only Anthony and Samuel had been missing to her, would she have still been negative and ordered me around like a maid? Was it only because the thought of losing her daughter that she had a change of heart?

I tried to imagine the thought of knowing all six of your children were dead. I knew from experience what if felt like to lose a brother and sister, but to lose the six children you had given birth to? I think Mother has changed just as it seems I have from this phenomenon.

I don't know what to do these days anymore. I do still worry, over Papa, but I don't need to worry about Nathan and Anthony and Samuel anymore, for Mother watches over them now. Bodies are still being burned, of course, but the finding of our parents seems to have enveloped out the world around A and S. They only smile and laugh and grin and tell jokes to Mother and sometimes Papa if he is awake and not delirious.

I wish I could laugh and smile like those carefree children. Sometimes I do, though by accident. Like when Vince says something funny or the boys play hide-and-seek with the one remaining rabbit Freddy. But then I clam up, remembering those suffering and the mass burnings taking place around the town and the disaster that surrounds us all.

Sitting with Papa. He is sleeping now, but when he was awake I told him the truth about his daughter Alice and son Edward. I told him Edward had run away—at least I thought—instead of going to the university. I told him Alice gave her life for the orphans.

Papa didn't say anything at first, only turned his head away from me. I asked him if he was all right.

"My last words to Edward were ones of anger," he said.

"Edward knew you loved him, Papa."

"Did he?" My father looked me in the eye, tears already streaming down his cheeks.

I made no answer, but let him weep without interrupting. I was cried out long, long ago, but somehow tears slowly started forming.

Tuesday, October 2, 1900

Papa still sick, but not nearly as bad as before. Seems we children cheered him up a bit. I would think so!

When the doctor comes and visits he rolls up Papa's pant leg and then examines the flesh. I caught a glance at it once. Part of the leg is slightly green. Then the doctor touches it with one of his tools, and Papa always moans in pain.

Sometimes the cuts on the leg reopen and start to bleed, and the doctor needs to wrap it in a bandage so they can heal.

Why is he not getting better? I want to ask. It has been more than a week, and his leg still hurts terribly. Will they have to amputate? Hopefully not. Maybe there is some *better* type of medicine they can give him.

Spoke with Clara Barton about Papa's leg. She thought a moment, then said, "Why don't you let me come see him? I might be able to help."

After we walked to the tent and she examined my papa, she said, "His fever is getting better, as is his delirium, but for some reason the infection in his leg is not going away." She tapped her lips, thinking. "Why don't we try putting more disinfectant on the leg, a couple times a day, while giving him more medicine for his fever, to prevent it from reoccurring."

So the nurses are doing as C.B instructed. First they take a wet cloth and dab it into boiling water, then cover Papa's leg with it. After a few minutes, they take the cloth off and disinfect the wound by applying turpentine. Lastly, they pour this medicine called Aloe Vera over all his cuts on the infected leg. Papa moans the entire time, his hands clenched around the bed-frame, knuckles turning white.

The nurses—dressed in white with only a single Red Cross pin attached below the shoulder—work quickly but thoroughly. Their lips are pressed together so tightly it looks as though they are glued together. Maybe they are trying not to sniff. I know I don't want to. With the burning of the bodies throughout the town and the dust and dirt and blood and rotting corpses, I wish I did not even have a nose.

Hopefully Papa will get better now.

Wednesday, October 3, 1900

No change.

Anthony and Samuel are just as playful as anyone can be these days. They run around the Red Cross camp, playing hide-and-seek, tag, and hopscotch. Samuel either hugs his rabbit to his chest while they do so or it is put away in a makeshift cage they made for it out of scrap wood.
      The nurses disapproved of the playing, since it was such a solemn time and now children were laughing and making jokes? But when they saw the smiles on some of the injured citizens, they stopped their argument and let A and S go. It is true. Those who are bloody and bandaged and still dazed take one look at my brothers and smile, sometimes even chuckle. Then the little children who had either been crying over the smell of burnt bodies or speechless with the disaster around them decided to join A and S. It is now a regular gang of six to nine year olds.

Anthony just looked over my shoulder and asked if I was writing about him. I said yes, and about his little gang. He asked, "Did you write down my friends' names? How are they gonna be famous and remembered if their names are never written down?"
      So here is a list of the Anthony and Samuel Gang:

Peter—nine years old; Mother died in hurricane; brown hair, blue eyes
Josiah—eight years old; Anthony's *best friend;* blonde hair, brown eyes; one brother died in hurricane; (twin with Josephine)

Josephine—eight years old; parents both alive; although a girl, A and S play with her quite often; blonde hair, blue eyes; (twin with Josiah)

Daniel—seven years old; talkative; black hair; parents alive

Catherine—six years old; really sweet; S likes to play with her; Father died in hurricane; very bright red hair and bright blue eyes

Theo—six years old; Samuel's *best friend;* brown hair, brown eyes; sister and brother died in hurricane; polite

There is the Anthony and Samuel Gang. At least my brothers can laugh and have fun, though, I fear, if I do so I am being disrespectful to those who have lost so much.

Friday, October 5, 1900

Miracle of miracles! This morning Papa wanted to sit up! He said his leg feels so much better. When the doctors came into check on him, I saw the green skin parts almost gone! No more infection! Thank you Clara Barton! That turpentine and Aloe Vera really work.

    A and S were so happy they jumped right onto Papa, not taking special care to beware of his leg. Papa didn't mind though. He just laughed and said, "My boys. Oh, boys." Nathan wanted in the group hug so he, too, wrapped his arms around Papa's neck, almost choking him.

    Watching them, I remembered the day when Alice had visited us for the first time since the move. How I had run to her and embraced her tight. Then how the whole entire family had bound out of the house and practically flattened her in a giant hug. I'll never get to hug Alice again. I don't have a sister. I am now the only daughter of James and Lillian Carson.

I ran out of the tent before anyone could see my tears. Only I bumped right into Vince. He saw me crying.

"What's the matter, Em? Is your papa all right?"

I nodded, trying to dry my face with my hand. "Nothing, Vince. Nothing's the matter. Papa is getting better. The medicine worked."

Vince let out a whoop, as if that had been his father in there and not mine. I laughed as I watched him dance around, forgetting all about Alice.

Sunday, October 7, 1900

Papa has improved so much he wanted to attend church services today.

This time, surprisingly, I wanted to go. I guess I have a lot to be thankful for now. My parents are alive when they could have been dead like so many others. I'm alive. Nathan, Anthony, and Samuel are alive. And I have two new friends—Vince and Clara Barton.

But though I thanked God for all those blessings during the mass, I couldn't help but ask Him, "Why did You even let it happen? Why did You take the lives of the orphans of St. Mary's Orphan Asylum and of the Sisters and Alice and Edward and thousands of others?" I received no answer. Maybe some day I will. Maybe some day I finally will know why God allowed such a phenomenon to happen and why he took Alice and Edward from me. But as for now, even though I am surrounded by death and destruction, I'm thankful.

Really I am.

Epilogue

Emelise Carson never understood why God had allowed the Galveston Hurricane of 1900 to occur, but when her father grew well enough to attend church services that October Sunday, and she saw how lucky she was to be alive after so many had died, she realized how truly thankful she should be.

Shortly after James Carson was well enough to travel, Emelise and her family moved back to Little Rock, Arkansas, unable to cope with the devastation that covered the once wondrous town of Galveston.

Emelise met up with Ruth Henry and found out the letter recording Edward's death had never arrived. Face to face, Emelise told Ruth of Edward's tragic death. Ruth lightly took the news, then told Emelise that while Edward was away, she had met Nicholas Simpson, a composer of music. Two years later they were wed.

Kate—Emelise's best friend—was overjoyed that Emelise was alive and well and had returned to Little Rock. She never asked Emelise to tell of her story about that fateful Saturday night, and Emelise never did, but Emelise did allow Kate to read her diary.

At the age of twenty-two, Kate married a mercantilist and moved to Connecticut, where she managed her own dress shop called *Kate's*. Even though hundreds of miles apart, Emelise and Kate exchanged letters and phone calls, remaining close friends for the rest of their lives.

Emelise also kept in contact with William Murney over the years—her first real friend since the move. After a few years, she found out by his letters that he had lied about his age and got a job at the railroad. Months later Emelise did not receive any word from him, and they eventually lost touch.

Through some research, Emelise was able to figure out the names of the Mr., Mrs., and young boy that had stayed at her house that Saturday night. She discovered that both the parents were killed in the hurricane, but the boy miraculously survived. He—Lucas—was sent to a Texan orphanage, where he remained there until a family adopted him. Later, he became a meteorologist on the Florida coast where he helped warn the citizens of oncoming hurricanes like Hurricane Annie.

James Carson was hired as an English teacher almost as soon as he arrived in Little Rock. He taught there for a total of thirty-five years. James never forgave himself for being so angry with his son, Edward. He often said, "If I never would have forced him to take those qualifying exams, he would still be alive." Although not a fact, James believed it. He became more gentle and understanding with is other children, letting them choose their own careers instead of him doing it for them.

James Carson died in his sleep at the age of ninety-three.

Lillian Carson, on the other hand, did not live as long as her husband. Only a few years after returning to Little Rock, she caught pneumonia and died a week later.

Though not a Catholic school, Nathan attended *The Institute for the Education of the Blind* in Arkadelphia, Arkansas, finishing one of the highest in his class. Well-known by his extraordinary talents with music, he was encouraged by the towns-people to take a career in it. He then traveled to New York City with Emelise and was accepted by an orchestra to perform piano. With some assistance at first, Nathan later remembered entire songs by memory and played them beautifully. Nathan remained in New York City his entire life, though he visited Emelise and his little brothers often.

Nathan's handsome looks caught the eye of one of the violin players—Annabelle. The two dated for a year, then were married in the newly constructed St. Athanasius Catholic Church. They had three children—Jesse, Raymond, and Pearl.

Nathan died in 1976 and Annabelle in 1978.

Pearl often visited her aunt Emelise, whom she was closest to, asking about the Galveston 1900 hurricane and taking notes, which she later published into a novel called, *One Survivor's Story of the Galveston Hurricane of 1900*. However, since only a few copies were printed, the entire manuscript was soon lost. Only the name of it is known.

Anthony and Samuel began their own animal clinic in Arkansas, taking in animals of all sizes, but mostly rabbits. They never did find their other two pets Fuzzy and Fluffy. However, Freddy lived to be a whopping fifteen years old, five years over the average life span.

They continued to collect and breed Californian rabbits over the years, entering them in state shows and winning numerous Grand Champions. Both Anthony and Samuel attended the same veterinary school in the same year—1911.

Only when World War I began in 1914, they dropped out of school and both signed up together on the same day. Anthony was sent to the France while Samuel was sent to Europe. Emelise wrote them almost every day, hoping and praying that they both would come home just as they had promised.

Samuel returned home to Emelise September, 1916, after he lost his right arm. It seemed only he had fulfilled his promise when neither a telegram nor letter arrived with word about Anthony, even when World War I had ended in 1918.

To the Carson family's complete surprise, Anthony arrived back in Arkansas in during the middle of a blizzard in January, 1919, without a scratch. A grin on his face and French mademoiselle's arm hooked through his as he bound through the door! He did indeed marry the young lady he brought home—Alexandrine Leclair. They moved to Massachusetts and had four children—Brigitte, Benjamin, Brice, and Bernadette. The four children each had two pet rabbits.

Anthony did not continue his education as a vet.

Anthony's wife died at the age of seventy and Anthony only a few months later.

Samuel, on the other hand, did go back to school and graduated a veterinarian in the early 1920s. He happened to be rescuing an injured dog a block away from his house when he met Ella. She was—to his great surprise—the daughter of a veterinarian. The two wed a few months after they met. They were unable to have children of their own, but they did adopt two daughters—Mae and Catherine. Samuel and Ella were both tragically killed in a motor car accident in 1935.

Emelise graduated from the University of Arkansas in 1911. She became a nurse for the veterans of World War I right there in Arkansas.

On May 21, 1915, Emelise was shocked to find out one of her new patients was a thirty-one year old man named Vincent. Unsure if it was really him, Emelise entered the man's room hesitantly. He had light brown hair and when his gaze met hers, Emelise saw those ocean blue eyes. Only when he grinned and said, "Top o' the mornin' to ya, Em," did she know it was really him.

Amazingly, Vince had signed up for the war in 1915. He was sent to travel on a ship called the *Charlotte*. Most mysteriously, in May, it exploded near Texas without cause or warning and Vince lost his left leg. Since most of the hospitals in that state were overcrowded with patients, he was transferred to the exact Arkansas hospital Emelise worked.

Emelise set herself to helping Vince use the crutches and make a full recovery, which he did.

After only a month of dating, Vince and Emelise were strolling through one of Arkansas's beautiful public parks when Vince stopped and bent down on his one good leg. He pulled out a jewelry box and opened it, revealing a dazzling ring. "Em?" he asked. "Are ya busy for the next fifty years or so?"

They were wed on July 17, 1915. They made their home in Little Rock, Arkansas, and had five children—Edward, Alice, Lillian, Julia (after Vince's mother), and Stephen (after Vince's father).

Emelise always felt bad that she was unable to give Alice and Edward a proper burial. To soothe her conscience, she and Vince purchased two tombstones and had them installed in the Calvary Cemetery in Little Rock. One is engraved: *Edward Carson; Loving Son and Brother; Killed in the Galveston Hurricane of 1900.* The other: *Alice Carson; Loving Daughter and Sister; Sacrificed her Life trying Save the Orphans of St. Mary's Orphan Asylum in the Galveston Hurricane of 1900.*

When Emelise was sixty-three, she returned to Galveston. Her breath was taken away when she stepped off the train and entered a colorful, bustling, extravagant town. No where were the destroyed houses and dead bodies that had once littered the street only fifty years ago. Instead, skyscrapers literally touched the clouds, cars of all types—old fashioned Model T's, Chevrolets, and even Bentleys—drove through the newly paved streets. People scurried in and out of shops, completely oblivious to the fact that only fifty years ago those same streets were littered with the corpses of previous residents.

Emelise returned home only after a week. She did enjoy admiring the newly constructed town, but she felt as though the people there had not treasured the lives lost decades ago. Emelise then wrote a letter to the mayor of Galveston asking for a memorial to be placed near the ocean to remember those who had died. Her wish was granted in 2000 when David W. Moore created a monumental bronze sculpture and installed it on the Galveston coast.

In 1978 Vince suffered a heart attack and was sentenced to his bed. Emelise, though she was an old woman, cared for her husband for three weeks while he tried to recover, but only grew worse. On a cold February evening, the two tightly held hands as Vince took his last few breaths. He finished with, "Top o' the evenin' to ya, Em," slowly closed his eyes, and breathed his last.

Immediately after Vince's death, Emelise bid herself to her bed, devastated. She died only hours after her husband, at the age of ninety-one.

When the new movers arrived in that Arkansas house two months later, one of the daughters—Mackenzie—happened to be rooting through the attic when she discovered a little brown book in a left-behind chest. It was the diary of Emelise Lillian Carson.

Twenty years later, Mackenzie traveled to Galveston, Texas, where she encountered secondhand the Hurricane of 1900 in the Galveston Historical Museum. Mackenzie did bring the diary of Emelise Carson with her, and, after some discussion with the owner of the museum and mayor of Galveston, permission was granted that the diary of Emelise Lillian Carson, written first hand during the Great 1900 Hurricane, would be on display in that museum. It is still there, the pages of that thirteen year old girl fascinating thousands of people for years to come.

Galveston, Texas 1900

Galveston and the Hurricane:

In the mid-19th century, Galveston emerged as an international city with trade coming in from all around the world. This city was one of the nation's busiest harbors, not to mention the world's leading haven for cotton exports.

Almost 38,000 people populated the island by 1900, the largest city in the country, in proportion with its size. It was no wonder that everyone wanted to live there. Galveston was a colorful, extravagant town with houses larger and more decorative than present day ones. Not to mention opera houses, fancy restaurants, and magnificent cathedrals and bath houses. The Galveston Bay and Gulf of Mexico surrounded the island, inviting anyone who wanted to to come and swim in it.

The threat of a hurricane did not worry the citizens, since there had only been a couple hurricanes in Galveston before. However, the citizens wanted to build a sea wall just in case. Famous meteorologist Isaac Cline wrote an article in the Galveston *News* in 1891 saying such a fear of hurricanes was an *absurd delusion.* He wrote, "It would be impossible for any cyclone to create a storm wave which could materially injure the city."

Isaac Cline would remember those words for the rest of his life.

The first signs of the 1900 hurricane were on August 27, 1900. Meteorologists waved it away like a fly. *No worries,* they said. *It's hundreds of miles away.*

But by August 31 the storm had entered the Caribbean Sea, and on Monday, September 3, it swept through Santiago, Chile. Simply in eight hours it had rained ten inches. By Friday, the total reached 24. 34 inches.

The cyclone began heading towards the southern parts of the United States. The winds reached twenty-eight miles per hour in Tampa, Florida. Meteorologists carefully examined the wind barometer. A barometer is used to measure the air pressure. If the reading is high, then the day will be clear. If the reading is low, then the day will be stormy. The average reading, at sea level, is around 29.92 inches. But that barometer had fallen to 29.42 inches. The meteorologist could not even begin to explain the rapid falling of the barometer. They knew it was a bad storm, but they insisted no cyclone could ever move from Florida to Galveston, so they tried not to worry about it too much.

By then near Louisiana the original twenty-eight miles per hour wind had increased to over a hundred.

First light Saturday morning, the sky was, as one citizen had described it, "…seemed to be made of mother of pearl, gloriously pink, yet containing a fish-scale effect which reflected all the colors of the rainbow. Never had I seen such a beautiful sky."

Only the residents of Galveston did not know that that sky would later turn pitch black within a few hours.

In the newspaper that day, an article had said, "The weather bureau had no late advances as to the storm's movement and it may be that the tropical disturbance has changed its course or spent its force before reaching Texas."

But that was not true.

Around eleven in the morning that day water from the Gulf began flowing down the street. It flooded yards a few inches. But the residents were not worried. Actually, they were very happy for the wind and rain, a relief from the hot summer.

Anonymous objects floated through the water: broken boards, small signs, toys. Hundreds of frogs were hopping through the water, trying to get onto dryer ground.

By 12:30 in some places the water had risen up to a man's knees. The rain felt like hail. No one grew nervous. Everyone enjoyed the day, some even falling down into the water-filled street and having the current carry them an entire block.

At one o'clock even downtown started to flood. Streetcars were no longer running and telephones no longer operating. By then, some residents had begun realizing the flood water was not from the rain, because it tasted like salt. The Gulf of Mexico and Galveston Bay were combining together.

2:30 PM Galveston time: a squall of wind had lifted the Weather Bureau's rain gauge off the Levy Building. It had captured a total of 1.27 inches of rain.

5:00 PM: the barometer fell to 29.05 inches.

5:15 PM: the wind had wrecked the bureau's anemometer. Before then the instrument had registered a total velocity of one hundred miles an hour.

5:19 PM: barometer at 28.95 inches.

6:48 PM: 28.73 inches.

Today, meteorologists record the lowest the pressure went to was 27.49 inches.

The wind measured 150 miles an hour, maybe even up to 200. Houses rattled and shook. Streets flooded. People drowned. Some of the residents of Galveston wished to head to the YMCA building, which they assured themselves it was much safer. And so it was, but most of those who attempted did not make it there. Most went unprepared, only worrying about the water that surrounded them than the wind that blew objects around like dust. Bricks blew around like feathers. Wood fluttered around as if it had wings. Decapitations occurred.

Later, around seven, the waves began rising incredibly high. Scientists still this day wonder why they went as high as they did. One witness said, "At one bound it reached my second story and poured into my door, which was exactly thirty-three feet above the street. The wind again increased. It did not come in gusts, but was more like the steady downpour of Niagara…" The entire island of Galveston was covered by a storm surge of up to 15.7 feet; the previous record from the 1875 storm was only 8.2 feet.

The next day, everyone was in a daze, as if half-dead. The smell of decaying bodies was so overpowering. Nothing was as it had been before. No more were the glamorous buildings and opera house and restaurants. Everything was either completely gone or partly destroyed.

Phillip Gordie Tipp, eighteen, had reached Galveston Sunday morning in a small sailboat. He said, "There were so many dead...we kept running into so many dead bodies that I had to go forward with a pike and shove the dead out of the way. There was never such a sight. Men, women, children, babies, all floating along with the tide. Hundreds of bodies, going bump-bump, hitting the boat."

The survivors began to wonder why no one had been warned about the Deadliest Hurricane in History.

Dead Gangs and the Mass Burnings:

On Monday men began stacking the dead bodies into carts and carrying them out to sea. Because the immune system in each of the bodies no longer functioned, bacteria could reproduce without being killed. It began to eat away at each person's cells, causing the decaying of the skin. Then the salty water began entering the bodies, and, as their cells were breaking down, the water could not be pumped back out, causing bloating of the stomach. No one in their right mind wanted to handle those disturbing beings. So soldiers rounded up fifty black men at gunpoint, forcing them to help with the tedious chore of weighting the bodies and then throwing them into the sea—all while temperatures reached the nineties, not to mention the intense humidity.

By late afternoon they had buried more than seven hundred bodies at sea.

Only the next morning at dawn hundreds of the bodies were back on the beach. Some had weights attached to them, some did not.

That left the soldiers and men with no choice. They again began rounding up the bodies, this time, however, for mass burnings throughout the town. Because of the decomposition, nobody wanted to handle the bodies. Soldiers pointed guns at those who refused to do the work. Some were shot.

Clarence Ousley, a worker of the *Tribune,* wrote, "It was realized that health, even the sanity of people in the streets, forbade the ghostly parade of carts to the wharf, and the only course was to bury or burn on the spot."

The quest of finding your loved one began to escalate. Survivors visited morgues and examined each decomposed face with uncertainty, wondering if they would ever find their relatives before the *disrespectful* Dead Gangs rushed in to burn them.

It is recorded that over a hundred bodies were uncovered from the wreckage each day and many began to say the confirmation of 6,000 dead was incorrect, and that it should be higher.

The Dead Gangs continued to burn the bodies until the middle of November, but the last body was found in February of 1901.

St. Mary's Orphan Asylum:

In the year 1866 Bishop Claude Dubuis sent out a message to missionaries which he named, *The Call.* Three French Sisters responded to the call and traveled on a boat to Galveston. They went with no one, knew no one, and did not speak the language.

Within a year after arriving, a sever epidemic struck, killing Sister Blandine and leaving Sister Ange crippled. But the one remaining Sister—Sister Joseph—persevered, and, after beginning St. Mary's Infirmary, began St. Mary's Orphan Asylum. In 1900, it was home to ninety-three children and ten Catholic Sisters. It was located only three feet from the Sandy Beach, but three *miles* from the city of Galveston itself.

There were two dorms, a boys' and a girls'. The girls' was must stronger because in 1875 a fire had destroyed it—no one was hurt—and a new one was built.

On the day of the hurricane, Sr. Elizabeth Ryan traveled to town to get some food for the orphans. Then she went to St. Mary's Infirmary. The Sisters there warned her about the oncoming storm and tried to convince her to stay, but she said, "No. I have the provisions in the wagon. If I don't go back to the orphanage, then the children will have no supper." But she didn't know whether or not she returned there would be no more suppers at the orphanage.

Meanwhile, the other Sisters at St. Mary's Orphan Asylum were watching out the windows, and, seeing the waves beginning to grow higher, decided to gather up all ninety-three children and put them in the second floor of the stronger girls' dorm.

The children pressed their noses against the window and watched as the giant waves began colliding onto the beach with much ferocity. They began to grow frightened.

The Sisters started signing the old French hymn "Queen of the Waves" to calm them. Then they heard the boys' dorm collapse next door. Thinking fast, the Sisters told Henry Esquior, an orphanage worker, to collect some clothesline rope. They tied the rope around the children's waists. Each Sister had between six and eight children tied together, and then tied to their own waist. One of the Sisters held two little children to her and said, "I'll never let go."

Water rushed into the first floor of the girls' dorm. They screamed, then began singing "Queen of the Waves" again. But they never finished the verses. The dorm was lifted off its foundation and drifted out into the sea. Some of the children looked out of the window in time to spot a giant ship come crashing into the side of the orphanage. The roof collapsed on the ninety-three children and ten Sisters.

All perished but three—William Murney, Frank Madera, and Albert Campbell. William Murney lost his little brother to the hurricane and he then woke up in a tree floating in the sea, the two other boys next to him. The three teenagers remained stranded for a day until fisherman came and rescued them.

When the Sisters' bodies were found, the six to eight children were still tied together and hooked to the women's' waist. One Sister was found with two small children tightly held in her grasp. Like she promised, she had never let go, even after death.

Clara Barton, Red Cross Camps, and More Help:

The Army sent soldiers with tents and food. One thousands loaves of bread arrived on the train-ferry *Charlotte-Allen* from Houston. Liverpool gave $13,580. New York gave the most at $93,695.77 while New Hampshire only gave a dollar. The Elgin Milkine Company of Elgin, Illinois, sent seventy-two bottles of its dried-beef, lemon and chocolate flavored, tablets.

Clara Barton and the Red Cross arrived September 17. Clara Barton, wrote, in one of her letters, "…the situation was not exaggerated."

She herself brought a trainload of carbolic acid and other disinfectants supplied by Joseph Pulitzer's New York *World*.

Clara Barton remained in Galveston until mid-November.

Reconstruction and Preparing for the Next Hurricane:

Reconstruction began almost immediately. Many wanted the disaster to be covered up and the horrid hurricane of 1900 to be forgotten and erased from memory.

But no one could forget it.

In 1903 the raising of the city began. Workers went around with white paint and marked a line on the telephones poles. That line showed the residents how much they would need to raise their house above the ground. Everything was raised: churches, stores, houses, mills. Even the 3,000 ton St. Patrick's Catholic Church was lifted five feet!

Construction began on the seawall September of 1902 and was completed July 29, 1904. It stretched 3.3 miles. However, it is now ten miles long, seventeen feet high, and sixteen feet thick at the base.

In 1915, a hurricane hit Galveston. It was almost as bad as the storm in 1900.

Only eight people from Galveston died.

Though there have been Hurricane Katrina, Hurricane Ike, and many others, the Galveston Hurricane of 1900 is still considered the worst historical event in US history. For more information about this hurricane, visit www.gthcenter.org.

Acknowledgments

    I would like my parents and my friends for reading my story over and over again as I continued to proofread it. I would also like to thank my Write Guide teachers, Ms. Finnigan, Dr. Siik, and Mrs. Rodenberg.

    Thank you Erik Larson, author of *Isaac's Storm,* for the inspiration your book gave me, and thank you ChillCover for the background that served as this novel's cover. And lastly, thank you Galveston and Texas History Center & Rosenberg Library for all the information on the Galveston hurricane!